THE BRUMBACK LIBRARY
OF VAN WERT COUNTY
VAN WERT, OHIO

Love's Sweet Echo

LOVE'S
SWEET ECHO

Louise Bergstrom

AVALON BOOKS
THOMAS BOUREGY AND COMPANY, INC.
NEW YORK

vs JY

PRINTED IN THE UNITED STATES OF AMERICA
BY HADDON CRAFTSMEN, SCRANTON, PENNSYLVANIA

Love's Sweet Echo

CHAPTER ONE

Early in the morning the beach on Mason Island was deserted except for the gulls and the quickly darting sandpipers that scattered as Gail approached, jogging happily along. It was impossible to believe that only yesterday morning she had awakened to see the snow of a late winter blizzard beating against her bedroom windows. Here in Florida the breeze felt soft, caressing, carrying with it the faint scent of some exotic flowering shrubs.

It had been a brute of a winter in Wallen, the upstate New York town where Gail Durand lived: one blizzard after another and many days of below-zero temperatures. After Gail's last bout of bronchitis, which had ended in pneumonia, her doctor had ordered her to get away for a while to a milder climate.

1

At first she didn't see how she could manage it. But then—like a miracle—an old friend of her aunt's, with a condominium on a small island off the west coast of Florida, had written to say that she was going to Minnesota for a little over two weeks to visit her daughter, and would they like to use her apartment while she was away?

Nora Halstead, Gail's widowed aunt, a former schoolteacher who had raised her after the death of her parents, had already signed up for a cruise with her travel club. But she insisted that Gail go down to Florida.

"Just what you need, child," she'd said. "A place in the sun without me around to hassle you."

Gail had been dubious about getting time off. She worked as a reporter and girl Friday on the town's newspaper, but it had been arranged quite easily.

"Go, girl, go!" the editor, Jim Watkins, had told her impatiently. "You look terrible—can't have you fainting all over the place. Besides, you have two and a half weeks' vacation time. Maybe you can send me some feature stories on upscale Florida living or something."

So here she was in Florida, pale and a bit wobbly, but delighted with everything she saw. Already the jogging had tired her, and she slowed to a walk. The pneumonia had certainly taken its toll of her strength. Ordinarily in good weather at home Gail ran several miles every morning before breakfast, but now, after so many weeks of illness, she was hopelessly out of condition.

She wondered how far she had come from the condo: a little over a mile perhaps. Mason Island was only a few miles long and never more than half a mile wide at any point. She must be getting near the bottom half. Judy Wood, the slightly plump, auburn-haired girl who worked in the condo office, had told Gail that half of Mason Island was privately owned by the Shane family, and they didn't care to have tourists wander into their territory.

Gail had seen a NO TRESPASSING sign nailed to a tree along the edge of the beach, but had ignored it. She was sure—well, almost sure—she had read somewhere that private ownership could not extend beyond the high-tide line on a beach, so where she was walking had to be in the public domain.

Gail's lovely brown eyes lit up with pleasure as she rounded a curve in the beach and found herself in a delightful little cove with a half-moon of soft white sand, exotically lined with swaying palms.

Charmed by the beauty of the spot, she dropped the towel she had draped around her neck, slipped out of her short beach robe, and headed for the water. An early-morning swim would be pleasant, she thought, after the jogging. And the water did indeed feel wonderful. She swam out beyond the breakers, then turned over on her back, gazing up at the sky where fluffy white clouds sailed like great clipper ships. Ah, this was the way to live, she thought.

Then it hit her—an incredible, paralyzing pain in her midriff that caused her to double over. Gail knew what it was; she'd had a cramp once as a child when she had swum too long in Lake Ontario. The main thing was not to panic. But the pain made her cry out, and her frantic movements made her sink beneath the surface.

In a moment she felt herself grasped by strong arms and turned onto her back, with a man's hand firmly beneath her chin.

"Try to relax," he said. "I'll take you in to shore."

The pain was easing off, and Gail tried hard to relax. "I had a cramp," she gasped. "It's almost gone now."

"It might come back if you try to swim. Just lie still and let me tow you in."

By now she was able to turn her head and take a look at her rescuer. All she could see was a wet blond head, a tanned, rugged, high-cheekboned face near her own, and a pair of blue-green eyes.

When they reached shallow water, he picked her up as easily as if she were a small child and carried her to the beach. Mixed with the embarrassment over her ignominious situation was a primitive delight in the touch of his bare skin against hers. It was as if an electric current flowed between them.

Her arms were around his neck, her face close to his. Then he set her down rather abruptly onto the sand.

"Are you all right?" he asked. His voice was cold, almost angry, as he gazed down at her.

"I—yes, I think so. Thank you very much," she stammered.

He was very tall, over six feet, with tanned, smoothly muscled limbs. He was wearing white bathing trunks.

"Obviously you're new here," he said, "so perhaps you don't realize how dangerous it is for you to swim alone. In the future I'd advise you to use the pool at the condo or wherever you're staying.

In any event, this cove happens to be private property. Didn't you see the signs?"

"But you don't own the Gulf!" she retorted indignantly. "Anything beyond the high-water line is public property!"

He didn't seem to be listening. Already he had turned and was striding away, over the low dunes toward the palms that lined the cove. She glared after him.

Who was he, anyway? One of the snooty Shanes, no doubt. Angrily Gail gathered up her towel, slipped into her beach coat, and started back the way she had come. She was very tired now, and it seemed to be a long time before she saw the buildings of the little beach settlement looming in the distance.

There were four condominiums, the first of which was called the Sand Dollar. That was where she was staying. There were also a few stores, a restaurant, and, farther along, several private homes. The island was connected to the mainland by a causeway, and there was a nearby town on the mainland—Crolby—that supplied most of the island's needs.

The Sand Dollar had a coffee shop and a swimming pool overlooking the beach, with a patio containing a number of tables and chairs under large beach umbrellas. There was a shower near the patio's back entrance for the benefit of those coming in from the beach.

Gail had just finished rinsing the sand off herself when she heard her name called. She looked over and saw Judy, the girl from the condo office, sitting at one of the tables drinking a cup of coffee and munching a doughnut.

"Want to join me?" Judy asked. "The coffee shop isn't open yet, but I can get you a cup if you'd like."

Gail went over to her and sat down in a metal chair. "Thanks, but I think I'd better go on up and get dressed. I'll come down for brunch later."

"You look a bit beat. Don't tell me you've been swimming alone in the Gulf!" Judy's friendly blue eyes widened.

"Yes, as a matter of fact, I did," Gail admitted. "And I got a cramp and might have drowned if a big blond Viking-type hadn't come along and pulled me out."

"Good grief!" Judy exclaimed. "That must have been Leo Shane! I've heard he's here now with his uncle."

"Well, he wasn't very pleasant. After he'd saved my life, he bawled me out for swimming alone and for trespassing on Shane territory. Just who is Leo Shane, anyway?"

Judy leaned back in her chair with a deep sigh. "Who is Leo Shane, she asks! Probably just one of the world's most eligible bachelors, that's all. For all the good it does us. He seldom comes out of his lair."

"What makes him so eligible? Aside from his physical attributes, I mean."

"Well, he'll probably inherit the Shane fortune when his uncle dies, and his mother is wealthy, too. She's Swedish and lives in a castle or something. He spends a lot of his time there with her."

"Tell me about these Shanes," Gail urged.

"Oh, they go back quite a way in Florida history. Once they owned this whole island, and a lot of land on the mainland as well. Owen Shane was one of the old wheeler-dealer types back in the land-speculation days. His parents had come here practically as pioneers when things were really primitive. Owen had two sons, Vince and John. John wanted to be a writer, so he went to Paris to get away from Papa and all that crass materialism. There he met and married a beautiful Swedish actress who was in Paris working on a film. This annoyed Papa Owen, who promptly disinherited John.

"But Vince was smarter. He pretended to be interested in Papa's real estate business and went to work for him. But as soon as the old man passed on to his reward, Vince took the money and ran. Became what they used to call an international playboy, you might say."

"Fast becoming an endangered species," Gail said. "What happened to John?"

"Ironically, he turned out to be the steadier of the two and was on his way to becoming a famous novelist when he died. His wife took their son, Leo, back to Sweden and later married a very wealthy Swedish nobleman of some sort who owned a big estate. He's dead, too, now and Leo runs the place for his mother. He just comes here for several months every year."

"So Leo is the only grandchild?"

"Unless you count Elizabeth, but she's not a blood relation. One of Vince's wives—the third, I think—had a daughter from a previous marriage, and Vince adopted her. I don't think Vince cared much about the kid, actually, and rarely saw her after the divorce."

Gail asked, "Where is she now?"

"In Hollywood, I think. She was always interested in acting. Finally, she married some foreign director. She's a few years younger than Leo, who's in his early thirties. I heard at one time there was a hot romance going between Leo and Elizabeth. But then she threw him over to marry the director. Maybe that's why Leo never married. And that, m'dear, is all I know about the Shanes. If you crave to know more, you'll have to do your own research."

Gail grinned. "Maybe I will. You're not a native Floridian, are you, Judy?"

"Goodness, no. I'm from Ohio. Came down to visit my uncle two winters ago and got hooked on the climate and the scenery. Since he manages the condo here, he offered me a job, and I stayed."

"What is your position here exactly?"

Judy shrugged. "Technically I'm assistant manager. But that's just a fancy name for doing a little of everything: receptionist, bookkeeping, cashier in the coffee shop in a pinch. I've even cleaned the pool on occasion. But I don't do windows!"

Gail laughed. "Sounds like my job. I'm supposed to be a reporter on a small-town paper, the *Wallen Chronicle*, but I do a little of everything, too. Not very exciting. I keep telling myself that someday I'll break away from Wallen and try for a job in the big city."

"New York? Well, you can have it. I'd rather be here in our little semitropical paradise. My boyfriend is a lawyer over in Naples, which isn't too far away. We're thinking of getting married this summer."

"That's great, Judy. You're lucky. I envy you."

"You mean to say you don't have a steady back home?" Judy's blue eyes were skeptical.

"Well, there's not too much choice in a little town. No one there has really rung my bell yet."

"Then maybe you should make a change. Is there anything to keep you in Wallen?" Judy asked.

"Not really. I live with my widowed aunt. I know she'd miss me if I left, but she's quite capable of looking after herself and has a lot of friends and activities, not to mention a sister in a nearby town."

"Well, a girl has to live her own life. My folks weren't too crazy about my moving down here, but they've accepted it." Judy sighed and drank the last of her coffee. "Guess I'd better get back to work. By the way, Gail, if you'd like to get out a bit while you're here, I'm sure Jeff could fix you up with somebody from his office. We could double-date some night."

"Thanks, Judy. Maybe later on. I'd just like to loaf and relax right now."

Gail went up to her apartment thinking about the Shanes. Jim Watkins wanted a story about upscale Florida life—maybe she could get something out of them. They sounded like an interesting family. But how could she make contact? Even though Leo had fished her out of the Gulf, he obviously didn't want any part of her.

Well, that was a challenge, and Gail liked challenges.

"Watch out, Leo Shane!" she muttered as she fished in her beach-robe pocket for the apartment key. "You are about to be infiltrated!"

CHAPTER TWO

The condo apartment was not very large—just one bedroom with a tiny kitchen off the combination living-dining room. But it was quite adequate for a woman living alone. Sliding glass doors covered most of one living-room wall. They opened onto a large balcony with a breathtaking view of the Gulf.

Gail had decided she would eat most of her meals on the balcony's outdoor table as soon as she laid in a few groceries. It would be too expensive to eat in the coffee shop all the time.

After she had taken a warm shower and rested a while, she went over to the little shopping center down the road and stocked up on a few staples. Then she fixed herself some lunch and lolled around on the patio. But in the late afternoon she began to feel restless and decided to take a walk.

Going down the short flight of concrete steps to the beach, Gail hesitated for a moment. Should she walk the other way this time—north instead of south? But that end of the island was too civilized. There were the condominiums and the motels and the houses. No, she preferred the unspoiled, jungly Shane half. And so she turned left and sauntered slowly along the beach. She had left her sandals on the steps because she loved the sensuous feel of the soft sand on her bare feet. Now she was wearing shorts and a T-shirt.

No jogging this time, just a leisurely stroll, looking for shells. Of course, if she happened to wander into Shane territory—well, they could only throw her out, she supposed.

Gail could feel the warmth of the sun through her thin shirt, although it really wasn't a hot day. In the low seventies. It was very pleasant, in fact, and a number of people were enjoying the beach.

However, once Gail had passed the Shanes' NO TRESPASSING sign, she found herself alone. But she went stubbornly on, telling herself that the Gulf belonged to everyone. The gulls wheeled and screamed above her, the sandpipers darted ahead of her, and suddenly she felt completely and irrationally happy.

This time when she reached the enchanting little cove, it was not deserted. A man was sitting in a short-legged beach chair under the shelter of a large umbrella: an emaciated, long-legged man who looked to be in his late sixties, with a rakish Vandyke beard and longish, thinning white hair, his eyes hidden behind dark glasses. Vince

Shane, no doubt, Gail thought, hesitating at the edge of the cove.

He looked up, saw her, and lifted a thin hand in greeting. "Do come and join me, my dear," he invited. "You've no idea how horribly boring it is just sitting here watching the damned sea gulls."

Gail laughed and walked over to him, seating herself in the sand beside his chair.

"I'm Vince Shane," he told her. "And who might you be?"

"Gail Durand. I'm spending my vacation at the Sand Dollar."

"Well, Gail Durand, welcome to Samburan."

"Samburan?"

"The name of our home here."

"It sounds vaguely familiar." She frowned, trying to remember. "Oh, I know! It's from that book by Conrad!"

"Fancy your knowing that. I didn't realize anyone read Conrad anymore."

"I was raised by a schoolteacher," she told him. "I've always adored Conrad. Why was your estate named after that place?"

Vince shrugged. "My father had a thing about the South Seas. He tried to make this little corner of Florida look as much like a South Seas island as possible. But tell me, why did you pick this lonely little key for your vacation? Most young people want to go where there's more action."

"The condo apartment was a loan. Anyway, I'm recuperating from pneumonia, so I need peace and quiet."

"Then we're two of a kind. I'm recuperating from a heart attack. Ordinarily, I'd be in the south of France this time of year. Actually, I hate Florida, but my nephew insisted."

"I think I met him this morning. I went swimming and got a cramp, and your nephew hauled me out. He also gave me a lecture about trespassing."

Vince made a face. "Never mind him! This place happens to belong to me, and you're welcome to come whenever you like. If your eyesight is good, you can see him out there now—in the Gulf."

Gail gazed out to sea and could just make out a blond head in the far distance. "And he had the nerve to tell me I shouldn't swim alone!" she said indignantly. "What if he got a cramp or a shark attacked him?"

"No shark would dare," Vince said dryly. "Well, here I am, and like the devious Mr. Jones in that Conrad novel, I bore easily. The price of a misspent life."

"Was it really misspent?" she ventured to ask. "I mean, if you've enjoyed it—isn't that all that counts?"

Vince Shane stared moodily at the sea. "But that's just the trouble—I haven't, really. Not after the death of my first wife. She was my real love, my only love. We had so many plans. We were going to run a small art gallery together. She wasn't a painter, but she knew art. Her father was an art expert. Only, she died giving birth to our child, and the child died, too. After that nothing ever seemed very important to me. I've led a restless, rootless life. I married again twice—but I could never recapture what I had lost."

"I'm sorry, Mr. Shane," Gail said gently.

"Oh, call me Vince, for heaven's sake. Well, it was a long time ago. But you remind me of Elsa —that was her name—with your head of dark curls, your big brown eyes, and the way you walk, with a sort of boyish grace, yet very feminine."

He grew pensive then and Gail felt a wave of pity for him. For all his money and worldly pleasures, he had often been lonely, she thought. And now he was facing death, and there was no one to hold him and keep the darkness away.

"It all goes so quickly, you know," Vince murmured. "One day you are young and have it all. The next day you're old and sick, and it's all gone —and you wonder, Gail. You wonder where it vanished."

"'The Bird of Time has but a little way / To fly—and Lo! the Bird is on the Wing,'" Gail quoted.

"Exactly. Old Khayyam knew the score, all right." Vince gave her an impish smile, shrugging off his somber mood. "Do you remember the rest of it? 'Come, fill the Cup, and in the Fire of Spring / The Winter Garment of Repentance fling.' You're lucky, Gail. The fire of spring is still burning for you—don't waste it!"

He was very easy to talk to, and she found herself telling him about her job on the newspaper and the recurring urge she had to get away.

"Of course," Vince said, "we all feel that urge when we're young. Don't fight it. Make a break, even if—oh, blast it, here comes Leo to spoil our fun."

Gail looked toward the Gulf and saw Leo coming out, looking like a rather indignant sea god.

"You again!" he exclaimed, glaring at her.

"Now really, Leo," Vince interposed, "Miss Durand is here at my express invitation. Must I remind you that Samburan belongs to me?"

Leo shook back his wet blond hair. "It's time for you to go in, Uncle. Come now." He pulled the umbrella out of the sand with a decisive gesture and closed it with a snap. Then he extended his hand to help the older man to his feet.

Gail scrambled up out of the sand. "I enjoyed talking to you, Mr. Shane," she told Vince with a warm smile.

"I told you to call me Vince. But you must come again. How about lunch tomorrow? I'd like to show you Samburan."

"I'm sure Miss Durand has better things to do, Uncle," Leo said coldly.

That did it. "On the contrary," Gail said sweetly, "I'd love to come. What time, Vince?"

"We usually eat at one." He allowed Leo to help him up. "Try not to be late. They make me rest in the afternoon."

"Fine. I'll be looking forward to it."

Leo gave Gail an annoyed glance, then picked up the beach chair. She watched as he and his uncle walked toward the palm trees. Vince looked back and waved before they disappeared. Gail started back along the beach toward the Sand Dollar. What was the matter with Leo Shane, anyway? she mused. Did he hate women, or was he just naturally disagreeable toward what he considered the lower classes? She intended to find out.

Judy was in the office when Gail got back, so she walked over to speak to her. The Sand Dollar had a large, attractive lobby with rattan furniture upholstered in brightly flowered material, a coffee table made from a slice of the trunk of some large tree, and many palms and other tropical plants in large pots. On one side were three self-service elevators. On the other side was a glassed-in cubicle with a desk and file cabinets where Judy was usually on duty. The coffee shop was at the back of the building facing the Gulf.

As Gail entered the office, Judy looked up from her typewriter.

"Hi! Where have you been?"

"Down the beach again. I wanted to see if I could get a glimpse of the Shane estate," Gail said.

"Good heavens, you really have a thing about it, don't you! You can't see the house from the beach. The island is very narrow down there and thickly wooded, and the house is over on the bay side—the inlet between the island and the mainland."

"Well, I'll see it tomorrow. As a matter of fact, I'm invited there for lunch."

"You've got to be kidding!" Judy exclaimed.

"No, really. Vince Shane was on the beach, and I had a nice talk with him. He was very friendly, and invited me to lunch tomorrow."

Judy shook her head. "I can't believe this. You've only been here a short time, and already you've accomplished something practically none of the local people have been able to do."

"Well, Vince and I just naturally seemed to hit it off," Gail said. "But that nephew of his is something else again! I think he'd like to throw me back in the Gulf to drown."

Judy eyed her thoughtfully. "Maybe he thinks you're after Vince, who has always had an eye for attractive females. After all, Leo has to think of his inheritance, you know. With his bad heart, Vince could go at any time—but suppose he decided to get married again? Disaster!"

Gail flushed. Did Leo Shane really think she was some kind of a fortune hunter? "He needn't worry," she said stiffly. "All I want out of the Shanes is a good story."

"Well, okay, honey, but be careful. Those Shanes are a tricky lot. You might find yourself a bit out of your depth."

"Nonsense! They're only people."

"Famous last words!" Judy said darkly. "Don't say I didn't warn you."

"No, I'll never say that, Judy."

Gail turned and left the office, heading for the elevators. She could still see Leo's blue-green eyes gazing at her with cold contempt. But when he had carried her out of the water, when he'd held his arms around her, he hadn't been cold then. He'd felt it, too, the exciting current flowing between them. She was sure of it!

How would he behave toward her tomorrow when she went to Samburan?

CHAPTER THREE

The next day Gail wondered what she should wear for her visit to the estate. Since everyone was very informal on Mason Island, she chose a pair of white shorts and a blue-and-white sailor jersey and put a pair of sandals in her beach bag.

Leo couldn't suspect she was trying to lure Vince in that outfit, she thought, inspecting herself in the big mirror on the back of the closet door. Whistling jauntily moments later, to quell the butterflies in her stomach, she began walking down the beach.

There was no one in sight at the cove this time, so she walked up the sloping beach to the row of palm trees, swaying gently in the late-morning breeze. Behind the palms was a heavy growth of semitropical vegetation. A path had been hacked through this jungle, and Gail followed it until she reached a clearing where the house stood in a green lawn, surrounded by trees and flowering shrubs.

It was not an imposing house, but it fit beautifully into its surroundings. Of white frame in the early-Florida style, it was two stories high and had a wide veranda that seemed to run all around it. There was a balcony on the second floor, and a big stone chimney. Gail went up the steps to the big front door and pressed the bell.

It was opened quickly by a tall, big-boned black woman in a spotless white uniform, who gave her a warm smile.

"Miss Durand? Come right in. Mr. Shane is expecting you." She had a faint Jamaican accent.

Relieved by this friendly reception, Gail followed her into a large hall that ran through the house, with a wide flight of stairs on the right. The maid led her along the hall and out a door onto the back veranda. Seated there in white wicker lounge chairs, sipping something cool, were Vince, Leo, and a big man with a head of shaggy red hair, a red moustache, and lots of bulging muscles. A short distance from the wicker chairs was a wood table set for four.

The men rose at Gail's approach and Vince came forward to take her hand.

"My dear, I'm so glad you could come!" He indicated the red-haired man. "This is Harry Fletcher, my nurse. Meet Gail Durand. And of course, Gail, you've already met Leo."

Harry nodded and stared at Gail with his rather cold green eyes. Leo gave her a little bow, his expression quite unreadable but at least not openly hostile. She was relieved to see that they were all wearing shorts and sport shirts.

"Sit down, Gail," Vince told her, "and have something to drink. I'm sure you're hot and tired after that long walk. I should have sent the car for you. I didn't think."

"Oh, no," she protested. "I love walking on the beach. It really isn't very far."

She sat down on a wicker lounge chair and the maid brought over a tray with a glass and a pitcher of fruit punch.

"This is Mary Forbes, who looks after us all," Vince said, and Gail and the woman exchanged smiles. "We'll have lunch in about ten minutes, Mary. That will give Gail time to cool off."

"Yes, sir." Mary poured some punch for Gail, put the tray on a small nearby table, and went quietly into the house.

"A lovely woman," Vince said. "Her husband, Floyd, takes care of the grounds and so on. They stay here year round to look after the place."

Gail sipped her cool drink, feeling rather uncomfortable sitting there with three men staring at her. Well, not really staring maybe, but looking anyway. While Vince chattered away about nothing in particular, she looked out beyond the veranda to where a green lawn sloped a hundred feet or so almost to the edge of the water that separated the island from the mainland. Here the water was quiet and peaceful, shimmering in the sun, with coconut palms curving gracefully over the edge of another narrow beach. Off to the left was a dock where a little cruiser was moored.

"I didn't realize the island was so narrow here," she remarked. "You have water close on both sides of the house."

"On three sides, really," Vince told her. "We're not too far from the tip of the key. Only, that end is mainly mangroves, so you can't walk around it. Actually, all the land on our half of Mason Island, except for the area around the house, has been pretty much left in a natural state. The Gulf side is better for swimming, but it is pleasanter to sit out here in the afternoon because of the sun."

"Yes, I can see that," Gail said. "I thought I could eat my dinner out on my balcony, but it gets the afternoon sun right on it, and there's too much glare. All the condominiums are built that way, facing the Gulf, and the view is wonderful, but you can't sit on the balconies until the sun gets low."

"Those condos never should have been built there at all," Leo said coldly. "A good hurricane, such as the one that hit here in '21, could dump them into the sea."

He sounded as though he wished one would, Gail thought.

"The lad's never forgiven me for selling half of Mason Island," Vince told her with his impish grin.

"It should have been left in its natural state," Leo said. "These little barrier islands are a shield for the mainland, but they shouldn't be built on. When they bulldoze away the dunes and protective vegetation, erosion destroys the beaches."

"But your house was built here, and it seems to have survived over the years," Gail objected.

"It was built on a rise—an old shell mound, actually," Leo replied, "and is about twenty feet above sea level. Also, it has the protection of the jungle. It's been damaged by storms, but has always survived because of its strategic location."

Mary was bringing lunch out to the table, so

they took their places around it. There was a lavish shrimp salad, fresh peas, a corn pudding, and hot rolls.

I won't need to cook any dinner this evening, Gail reflected, taking a bite of the delicious shrimp salad.

The conversation turned to the past and present Indians of Florida.

Leo, an expert on the subject, gave a short lecture on the Calusas and others, finishing with, "It would be very complicated to try to explain the various tribes who came to comprise the present Seminoles."

"Well, don't even attempt it, old boy," Vince said cheerfully, grabbing the center of attention for himself. "We don't want to bore our guest, you know." Then he began an amusing anecdote about a party he'd once attended on the Riviera, and Leo lapsed into silence.

Harry ate a great deal and seldom spoke, although Gail was aware of his eyes on her from time to time. She thought that he didn't look much like her idea of a male nurse. Bodyguard would be more like it.

For dessert there was a luscious pecan pie, and Vince complained bitterly because he had to eat plain custard instead.

When the meal was finished and they had left the table, Vince said: "And now, my dear, you'll have to excuse me. Harry is quite adamant about my rest period. But Leo will show you around the place, I'm sure, and take you home later."

Gail was shocked at being so summarily thrust upon a man who obviously wanted nothing to do with her.

"Oh, that isn't necessary," she protested. "I'll just walk back along the beach to the Sand Dollar. Thank you for a lovely lunch."

"Nonsense, my dear. Leo can drive you. He probably has some errands to do, anyway. And you'll come back to see me again tomorrow, won't you? I'm usually on the beach in the morning. There's really no place else to go."

"I'm not sure," she began hesitantly.

"Oh, but you must! There's something I want to talk to you about. Please don't fail me."

Vince allowed Harry to lead him off before she could think of a polite way to say no. After all, there was no point in getting too involved with him, and she didn't want him to get any wrong ideas.

As she stood there, rather at a loss, Leo said: "Don't let my uncle pressure you, Miss Durand. He can be rather high-handed at times when he wants something. If you'd rather not come, just say so and I'll give him the message."

You'd like that, wouldn't you? she thought. Obviously Leo would prefer that she never came near Vince again. Well, she wouldn't give him the satisfaction of such an easy victory.

"I like to walk on the beach, anyway," she told him a bit haughtily, "so it's no hardship to spend a little time with your uncle. I think he's lonely."

Leo's lips tightened, but he made no further attempts to dissuade her.

"Come inside then, if you want to see the house," he told her.

They went inside to the big living room that ran the length of the house. It was a beautiful, gracious room with a big stone fireplace, some excellent paintings of local scenery, casual rattan furniture, and hand-woven rugs on the polished parquet floor. Built-in bookcases on either side of the fireplace were filled with books that looked well read, and at one end of the room there was a baby grand piano.

"It's charming!" Gail exclaimed. "Do you spend much time in Florida, Mr. Shane?"

"Several months every winter."

"And the rest of the year you live in Sweden?"

"Yes, at Rosenborg with my mother. Since her husband died, I help her manage it."

Gail would have liked to question him further, but the aloof expression in his blue-green eyes was not very encouraging. Better to let him finish the tour and take her home as soon as possible.

What was the matter with him, anyway? she thought angrily. And why did he have to be so—so darn attractive!

He led her across the hall to a formal dining room with big windows facing the Gulf.

"We only eat here in bad weather," he said. "Next to this there's a library which we have converted into a bedroom for my uncle, since he's not supposed to climb stairs. Off that is a small office where Harry sleeps in case he's needed during the night."

"Is your uncle very ill?" Gail asked.

Leo hesitated, as though debating just how much he should tell her. "He had a slight heart attack, but he's much better now. However, we have to keep a close eye on his activities."

Such as picking up strange females on the beach, Gail thought dryly.

They went up the wide staircase to the second floor. Here there were two bedrooms at the front of the house with a view of the Gulf, and two at the back. All the rooms had French windows that opened onto the screened balcony. Each of the rooms also had a private bathroom.

"Originally, there was only one bathroom upstairs and one down," Leo said. "But Uncle added the others. In America people seem obsessed with plumbing facilities."

"It's a very comfortable house," Gail told him. "It seems to belong here in a way the condos never could."

His face darkened. "They certainly don't belong here. But you'll find them all along the coasts of Florida. It's not only stupid but dangerous. A good hurricane could destroy them. Now this is not a pretentious house, but it does fit into its environment. I love it and have always enjoyed staying here."

They went downstairs and Leo showed Gail around the grounds, which were more extensive than she had realized. There was a four-car garage with an apartment over it where Floyd and Mary Forbes lived. It contained three cars: a silver Mercedes, a pickup truck, and a Toyota.

From the garage a driveway curved off to join a narrow road leading north through the jungle.

"Once," Leo told Gail, "the whole island was just wilderness, and the only way to reach it was by boat. But after half of it was sold, the developer came in with his bulldozers, cleared out half of the jungle, and built a causeway to the mainland. Now it's no longer private."

Gail could tell by his voice and the wistfulness

in his eyes that he still grieved for the lost wild beauty.

"Sometimes I get the feeling that the bulldozer is the Minotaur of the twentieth century," she said lightly, "the monster waiting at the end of every labyrinth!"

Leo gave her a surprised glance, as though the stupid child had suddenly shown evidence of intelligence. Then he smiled.

"Yes," he said. "Quite so." He turned toward the garage. "Would you like to go home now?"

Gail realized she was being dismissed. "I can walk," she said stiffly.

He looked at her. "I'm sure you can. But I have an errand in town, anyway."

There was no point in not riding with him, so Gail followed him over to the cars. He opened the door to the Mercedes to help her in. At least he had good manners, she thought, whatever else he might lack.

They drove along the narrow road, and Gail saw that there was a great variety of trees and plants on both sides.

Noting her interest, Leo said, "My grandfather was fascinated by tropical vegetation and brought in specimens from all over the world." He pointed out various trees and shrubs.

Gail, too, was fascinated by the exotic vegetation, but every now and then she looked at Leo's hands on the steering wheel. They were big but slender, strong-looking but shapely. Hands that could be tender. Gail tried to force her thoughts away from Leo Shane. No matter how strong an attraction she might feel for this man, he was obviously not for her.

Finally, they reached the end of the wilderness area and came to a stone wall with a wrought-iron gate. Leo stopped the car.

"To keep out tourists?" Gail asked as he got out of the car to open the gate.

"After the causeway was built," he told her, "young people from the mainland would drive over, and this became a popular lovers' lane. If we hadn't put up a barrier, our road would soon have been knee-deep in beer cans and other debris."

From the wrought-iron gate it was only a short distance to the Sand Dollar. Leo turned into the drive and pulled up in front of the entrance. Before getting out to open the door for Gail, he sat for a moment looking at her.

Then he said: "Do you intend to visit my uncle again tomorrow?"

She could feel her hackles begin to rise. She had been thinking that she ought to break off her association with the elderly man before it became awkward, but now she said, "I think so. I enjoy talking to him and, as I said, I believe he's lonely."

"He's not lonely, Miss Durand," Leo said. "He's bored. There is a difference. A difference that can sometimes be dangerous. I can't prevent your seeing him, of course, but I would sincerely advise against it."

He came around to open the car door for her, and she slid out, looking up at his imposing height. For a moment the feeling she'd had on the beach when he'd carried her out of the water swept over her—a feeling so intense that it was almost visible, like a flash of electricity. With an effort Gail turned her eyes from his.

"I see no possible harm in it," she told him. "Thank you for bringing me home, Mr. Shane."

She watched him drive away, then turned in a daze to enter the building.

Oh, yes, she thought. Yes, she would certainly go to Samburan again.

CHAPTER FOUR

That evening after a very light meal, Gail went down to sit on the patio by the swimming pool. The sun was low and all the bathers had left. Judy came out and sank into one of the lounge chairs beside her.

"Hi! I've been dying to talk to you. How was your visit with the Shanes?"

"Interesting," Gail replied and went on to describe the house and the meal and Vince's rather peculiar nurse.

"I see him driving by occasionally," Judy said. "Not a friendly type. Doesn't talk to anybody around here."

"The house was much more modest than I expected," Gail said, "but very charming."

"Well, of course, it's no mansion like some of

the early millionaires built, but then at that time the Shanes weren't all that rich, I guess."

"I wonder why Vince sold part of the island," Gail mused. "Surely he didn't need the money."

"I wouldn't know." Judy shrugged. "Maybe he just wanted to liven the place up. But tell me about Leo, the inscrutable Swede. I saw him bringing you home. Did he make a pass?"

"Good heavens, no!" Gail exclaimed. "He just wants to get rid of me. I wonder why? I can't see that I'm any sort of threat."

Judy looked at her thoughtfully. "Vince seems taken with you, from what you say. Maybe Leo's afraid he might want to get married again—and there would go his inheritance!"

Gail said, "Vince is old enough to be my grandfather! I'd never marry for money, anyway."

"But Leo doesn't know that. And the women around here are always scheming to meet the Shanes. You've no idea!"

Gail felt her cheeks flame. So Leo thought she was just a fortune hunter! Maybe he even thought she'd faked the cramp to get him to rescue her! What a revolting idea! Perhaps it would be better if she never saw any of them again.

"Oh, by the way," Judy continued, "there's a dance at the yacht club next Saturday and Jeff said he could get a date for you if you'd like to go with us. We go nearly every week. It's not as ritzy as it sounds. You don't have to own a yacht to belong. It's really nothing but a country club with a marina, and everybody around here belongs. How about it?"

Gail hesitated. "Is it formal? I didn't bring any really fancy clothes along."

"Heavens, no. Oh, some of the older women get

all gussied up, but the college kids come in jeans. They only draw the line at bare feet. A couple of times a year they have a formal dinner dance, but these Saturday night affairs are very casual."

"Well, all right, thank you, Judy. I'd like to go. Do—do the Shanes ever go there?"

Judy gave Gail a hard look. "Vince used to, but not since his heart attack. Leo—well, they say he used to go there with Elizabeth, but not anymore. So I doubt if we'd run into him. Well, I've got to go in. I'm supposed to be on duty in the office. See you later."

Gail lingered outside a while, watching the sunset over the Gulf. It put on its usual flamboyant display: streaks of peach and coral and gold against the blue background. Unlike the northern sunsets, however, it was very brief, fading within moments of reaching its peak.

Like life, Gail thought. A blaze of glory, and then darkness. She sighed, feeling very sad.

Around ten o'clock the next morning Gail put on her bathing suit and beach coat, picked up her canvas bag, and started off once more along the beach. When she reached the cove, there was Vince on his beach chair. He looked up and waved eagerly as she approached. She sank onto the sand beside him.

"I was afraid you might not come," he said.

"Why wouldn't I?" Gail said.

"Well"—he grimaced—"there was a chance Leo might have talked you out of it. Blasted young idiot. I'm not supposed to see anybody or do anything that might excite me. Might as well be dead and be done with it. It's like being in prison."

"But you are getting better, aren't you?" Gail asked soothingly. "It won't be like this forever."

"I certainly hope not. Yes, I'm getting better. But I've got to have some amusement, to be involved in something. That's what I wanted to talk to you about, Gail. For some time I've been thinking that I'd like to write my memoirs. I've had an interesting life, known a lot of famous people, and I've got a lot of material: letters, journals, clippings, and so on, to refresh my memory. I keep it all right here in this house, because it's the only real home I have. When I travel, I usually stay in hotels. I've never made a practice of buying houses in various countries the way some people do. Too much trouble to keep them staffed and maintained. I've got a chest in my room here full of memorabilia."

"It sounds like an excellent idea," she said.

"But the trouble has been that I've always been too busy to get down to it. Now I have all the time in the world, but I lack the energy."

"You could get somebody to help you," she suggested. "A secretary or—"

"Exactly." Vince pulled off his dark glasses and looked at her with eager eyes. "Talking to you, Gail, has brought back the old urge to get it all down before it's too late. You are just the person I need to help me!"

She stared at him in astonishment. "Me, Vince? I'm not a secretary, and I already have a newspaper job back home."

"You can type, can't you?"

"Yes, but—"

"And you're better than a secretary, you're trained to write. That's what I need—sort of a ghost writer, I suppose. I never had any talent for it myself. But together we could do it! Didn't you say you wanted to get away from that small town? We could get it started here. And as soon as I'm well enough, we could go to France to finish it—or anywhere you'd like. I don't know what you're earning in the job you have, but I'll double it. And if the book is published, we'll split the profits. What do you say?"

He looked so happy and excited over his proposal that Gail hated to throw cold water on it. But she could hardly just walk out on her old life and stay here. Especially since the new job would be only temporary. Vince would probably grow bored with the whole project after a few weeks, and what then?

"Vince, I don't know if—"

"Oh, of course, you couldn't agree to do it just like that. You'll need time to think about it. Take the rest of your vacation to decide, if you need to. And in the meantime, I'll get out the material and we can go over it someday. The idea does have some appeal to you, doesn't it?"

"Of course it does, Vince. But I feel overwhelmed. It's too big a decision to make on the spur of the moment, as you say."

"But you will promise to think about it?"

"Yes, I will," Gail said.

"Good! That's all I ask."

She didn't stay with him on the beach very long that day; she wanted to be alone, to think about his offer. The whole thing was really ridiculous, she told herself as she walked home. He was probably too ill to take on anything like that; it was just a whim. And she was a journalist. She couldn't throw over a perfectly good job for something so chancy.

And yet if she did stay on Mason Island, she could remain near Leo. Which, of course, was the worst thing she could do! He probably wouldn't let Vince hire her, anyway. But could he stop his uncle? She suspected Leo would be furious about the whole thing, if he knew. Maybe she ought to accept just to spite him!

But what was she thinking of? Of course, she couldn't accept. Could she? Gail's heart was beating with wild excitement at the new vistas opening up before her. Yet she couldn't reach a decision.

For the next two days she stayed away from Samburan, wanting to clarify the situation in her mind. No matter how good Vince's offer sounded on the surface, Gail had some nagging doubts about it.

Then on the evening of the second day, her telephone rang. She expected it to be Vince, wondering why she hadn't been down the beach to see him. But it was his nephew.

"Miss Durand? Leo Shane here. I have to drive up to Naples in the morning around nine, and I thought you might like to go along, since you haven't seen much of the area yet."

For a moment Gail's heart was flooded with joy, but then came doubt. Had Leo found out about Vince's offer, and did he intend to talk her out of accepting it? Well, what if he did? She didn't have to let him influence her if she didn't want to—and at least she would have a few hours with him, even though she knew nothing could come of it.

"Why, thank you. I'd like to go."

She hung up the phone moments later and gazed out the glass doors to the Gulf. What had made her accept Leo's invitation? she wondered. He obviously didn't like her. She had to get over the ridiculous crush she had on him! She was old enough to know better.

Gail suddenly remembered what she had said to Judy about nobody back home ringing her bell. Well, Leo rang it, she thought wryly—loud and clear! For all the good it would do her. He might as well have worn a NO TRESPASSING sign around his neck like the one at the edge of the Shane property.

Gail was waiting in the lobby promptly at nine the following morning wearing a beige pleated jersey and a brown silk scarf held in place with a gold pin. Her dark curls were brushed into a shining cap, and her skin had a warm golden glow from all the sun she had been getting.

Leo came in and his eyes held a gleam of approval as he gave her his slight European bow.

"Good morning, Miss Durand."

He was wearing pale-yellow slacks and a white sport shirt, and simply glowed with an aura of masculine appeal. She wished that the sight of him didn't affect her so strongly.

"Good morning," she said. "Do you have to be so formal? You could call me Gail, you know." The instant the words were out, she was shocked by her boldness.

He smiled and took her arm. "Very well, Gail."

As they walked out to his car, she asked, "How's Vince today?" Then she bit her lip; he'd think Vince was all she was interested in. Would she keep saying dumb things all day?

"About as usual. He's chafing because he wants to get back to his old life, but I doubt that will ever be possible."

Whatever his life might have been, Gail thought. Wine, women, and song? Change the subject, forget Vince.

"I haven't been off the island since I got here," she told Leo, "so this will be a nice change."

"How did you come in?"

"A shuttle flight from Tampa to Naples, and a taxi from there. It was dark by the time I drove over from the airport, so I didn't see a thing. It seemed a short distance."

"It's only about nine or ten miles. We're rather off the beaten track, though. South of us the only town is Everglades City on the edge of the National Park."

"I'd like to see something of the Everglades while I'm here," Gail said.

At least Leo was being polite and friendly, not treating her like an enemy, as he'd done in the beginning, she thought when they turned onto the causeway.

Aloud, she said, "I guess it must be a lot more convenient for you being able to drive on and off the island than it was in the old days."

"Convenient, yes, but I preferred it when we used a boat. We kept our cars in a garage near a dock on the mainland, so it really wasn't much different. The blasted causeway is useless in a storm, anyway—always underwater. If there is ever another bad hurricane—and there will be— they would have to evacuate the people who live here hours ahead of time."

"Have you ever been on the island during one?" Gail asked.

"No, because we were only here around the winter, but I've often heard about the really bad one in '21. The island was mostly underwater, except the area where our house stands. All the trees blew down and the house was somewhat damaged, but it survived. My father was here then. And when I was a little boy, I loved to have him describe it. Vince was here, too, but he was pretty young, so he doesn't remember it too well. Of course, we've had some pretty good ones since then. But that was the worst."

"How old were you when your father died?" Gail asked.

"Eight. Until then we lived in Paris. But after my grandfather died, we would come here every winter for a few months. Even after my father died, we continued to come—until my mother married again. After I was grown, I continued to come on my own. I love this place."

As long as he was answering questions so willingly, Gail thought, she would continue to ask them. "Do you prefer living in Sweden to living here?"

"Not really, but running the estate is a challenge, and my mother depends on me since my stepfather's death."

"Where is the estate located?"

"In southern Sweden, just across the straits from Denmark."

It was a beautiful day, neither too hot nor too cold. And they seemed to reach Naples all too soon.

"Twenty years ago this was just a sleepy little retirement town," Leo told Gail. "Now it's a bustling city full of high rises and crowded with traffic and tourists."

Gail was beginning to get the idea that he hated any sort of progress, but such an attitude seemed futile to her. The world kept changing, and there wasn't much you could do about it. She could understand how Leo felt, however. Naples was a very pretty little city, but it must have had more charm in the past. Luckily, the main street still ran straight down to the beach, and there were lots of palm trees and flowering shrubs growing everywhere.

With some difficulty, Leo found a parking spot. "I'm not sure how long my business will take," he told Gail, "but I thought it would be a chance for you to walk around and look at the shops. I'll meet you back here in about an hour."

He strode off and she saw him disappear through the door of an office building. She turned her attention to the shops, some of which were very chic indeed and looked expensive. It would be fun, she thought, to buy something, but she probably couldn't afford much at the prices they most likely charged.

She wandered along, gazing in the windows at souvenirs made of shells, as well as expensive shoes, swimsuits, and evening gowns. In one of the clothing stores Gail saw a dress that looked as though it might have been made just for her: a pale-gold, ankle-length chiffon with a fitted bodice and a full skirt.

She stood for a moment, eyeing it wistfully. She could wear that to the yacht-club dance. Of course, Judy had said Leo didn't go there anymore, but you never knew.

On an impulse Gail went into the shop. When she asked a saleswoman the price of the dress in the window, the woman said: "You're in luck, dear. It just went on sale today—half price. End of the tourist season, you know."

Even at half price it wasn't cheap, but Gail impulsively said, "I'd like to try it on."

The dress fit her perfectly, making her look and feel quite glamorous.

Well, she thought, if she did take the job with Vince, she could afford it. But was she going to take the job? Gail knew now that she wanted to—terribly. Because it would mean seeing more of Leo.

She walked out of the shop a few minutes later carrying a fancy black-and-silver box, feeling curiously elated. Her first step toward a new and more exciting life, she thought. After that she hardly dared look in the other shops, although she did buy her aunt a handsome wallet and a box of writing paper decorated with scenes from Florida. In addition, she bought herself a couple of paperbacks.

When Gail went back to the car, Leo was already there, reading a newspaper.

"Did I keep you waiting?" she asked, sliding in beside him.

"No, I just got here, and I was a few minutes early." He glanced at the box in her lap. "I see you've been shopping."

"I got a new dress. I thought I'd wear it to the yacht club Saturday night."

He regarded her with some surprise. "You are going there?"

"Yes, Judy Wood, the niece of the manager of the Sand Dollar, is getting me a date."

"I see." Leo didn't look altogether approving. "A blind date. Isn't that what you call it?"

"That's what you call it. After all, I don't know anybody here," Gail said defensively.

He backed the car out to the street. "I thought

we could drive up the coast a piece to have lunch before we go back," he said. "Do you like seafood?"

"Love it."

"Good. I know just the place."

They returned to the busy highway, but after a while Leo turned off on a side road leading to the Gulf.

The restaurant turned out to be a rustic little place called The Fish Shack. It was built on a pier over the water near a marina. They sat outside under a thatched roof at a plank table where they could watch the boats going in and out of the marina. They could also watch the pelicans waiting for a handout from one of the fishermen cutting bait or cleaning a catch. Such ungainly birds, Gail thought, yet so graceful in flight.

The air smelled strongly of the sea and fish, and she inhaled it as though it were rare perfume. Leo looked relaxed and happy as he sat back watching the pelicans, the wind blowing his fine golden hair about his lean face. They ate big helpings of shrimp and crab cakes, the specialty of the place, and he talked to her, inquiring about her life, her work, her plans for the future. He seemed interested and sympathetic, quite different from the cold, unfriendly man he had seemed in the beginning.

"I've decided," Gail told him, "that I don't want to stay in a small town all my life."

"There is nothing wrong with small towns," Leo said. "The best of life can be found in them."

"But I want to see the rest of the world!" she protested. "Just coming down here has made a difference in the way I feel. It's all so new and beautiful!"

"But after a few years it would be just another small town," he said with a shrug.

Finally, over cups of the best coffee she had ever tasted, he regarded her with a serious, intent expression and said: "Gail, are you going to take the job my uncle has offered you?"

She felt a cold lump form in her stomach. So here it was—the reason for the nice lunch and all the pretended sympathy.

"Did he tell you about it?" she said. A stupid question, she thought angrily. How else would Leo know?

"Yesterday I found him going through all the piles of old papers he keeps in a chest. When I asked him what he was looking for, he said he was planning to write his memoirs and that he had asked you to help him. He also said you hadn't given him an answer yet. Is that correct?"

"Of course, I couldn't decide on anything that drastic without giving it a lot of thought," she replied.

"No, I don't suppose you could." Leo leaned back in his chair and regarded her thoughtfully. "You know, Gail," he said, "when we first met, I thought you were just another of the silly girls who try all sorts of tricks to get involved with the Shanes."

"I suppose you thought my drowning was staged."

"At first, yes."

"But not now?" she asked.

"No, not anymore. You're too sensible and intelligent to play that sort of trick."

"Thanks a lot. But what do you think I'm up to then?"

"I don't think you're up to anything, Gail, except perhaps to get a story for your paper."

She winced. Actually, she'd forgotten she'd ever had that in mind.

"It's what my uncle is up to that concerns me," Leo went on.

"Isn't he rather too old and ill to have evil designs on me?" she asked dryly.

"Vince is a strange man, Gail," he said slowly. "I have never really understood him. There's a great deal more to him than what appears on the surface."

"Isn't that true of anyone?" she said.

"Yes, but not everyone is...dangerous."

"Dangerous?" Gail repeated incredulously. "Surely you don't expect me to believe that?"

Leo sighed. "I suppose not. He's too darn charming. It's easy to be taken in by him. Women have always adored Vince. He talks a great deal about the great tragedy of losing his first wife and their baby—yet he married two more times and has had many romances."

"But perhaps all that was just a vain effort to regain his lost happiness," Gail protested.

Leo's blue-green eyes probed hers. "He would certainly try to make you believe that, at any rate."

Taking out a pack of cigarettes, he offered her one. When she refused, he lit one for himself.

Then he continued. "All this talk about writing his memoirs—that's just nonsense. Vince wouldn't stick to it more than a few weeks. He bores easily, you know. You may be tempted to accept his offer because you're convinced he's a lonely, unhappy man, and because you're in just the mood for a change of lifestyle, an escape from what you consider a humdrum existence."

"I still don't see—"

"It would be a disaster," Leo told her firmly. "I'd rather not explain why, but please believe me, Gail. It could be a total disaster. I am asking you to refuse any offer he might make, however attractive it may seem."

There it was, laid on the board. In another minute he would be offering her money never to see Vince again, the way fathers did in old-fashioned novels. Her cheeks flushed with anger.

"I find it difficult to believe you would go to all this trouble to protect me, someone you barely know," Gail said. "It is much easier to believe that you're concerned about yourself, your own future. I know that your father was disinherited and that Vince got all the Shane money. Miraculously he got rid of all his wives and had no offspring, unless you count the adopted daughter. So no doubt you will be his heir—unless he should marry again in his final years. Isn't that really what you're afraid of, Leo—that he might offer me marriage and that I might accept it to get the freedom I long for? Isn't that why you brought me out here and stuffed me with crab cakes and kindly talk? You're scared silly that you might lose your inheritance!"

Gail stopped for breath, glaring at him. She expected Leo to react with equal anger, but to her astonishment he laughed with genuine amusement.

"If you only knew how funny that is!" he said, stubbing his cigarette out in the ashtray. "You've certainly picked up a lot of gossip in the short time you've been here. Well, I'm not going to bother denying anything—you wouldn't believe me anyway—but please take my word for it that the situation is much more complicated than you realize."

"It doesn't matter what I believe, Leo. I'll make my own decision, and don't think you can frighten me off with any vague hints."

He sighed. "Then you are going to accept Vince's offer?"

Was she? Gail still didn't know. But after Leo's blatant attempt to head her off, could she just turn around meekly and say, "Very well, sir, from now on I'll have nothing more to do with the Shanes."? No, she couldn't!

"I probably am," she said coldly.

CHAPTER FIVE

On Saturday morning Judy came up to Gail's apartment while Gail was fixing breakfast and said: "You haven't forgotten about the date tonight, have you? Jeff told me he's got somebody nice lined up, so I hope you haven't changed your mind."

"No, I hadn't forgotten. What time will we leave?"

"The guys will pick us up around seven. Don't eat anything before we go, because they have a buffet supper at the club and they put out a pretty good spread."

"Okay, Judy. I'll be ready," Gail said.

As the day slowly passed, she was glad that the coming evening at the yacht club loomed ahead of her. It helped take her mind off the Shanes and the way they were both complicating her life. Al-

47

though she had told Leo she was going to take the job with Vince, Gail still wasn't sure if it was the right thing to do. After all, it might turn out to be very temporary indeed, and then where would she be?

Oh, forget about the Shanes for today, Gail ordered herself. Then she spent several hours experimenting with her hairdo and makeup. Finally, she showered and put on the new dress. It really did something for her, too. Very attractive. She wore a gold locket with it.

Then Gail wondered why she was going to so much trouble to look her absolute best. She certainly wasn't that eager to impress her blind date or the people she would meet at the yacht club. It was just a compulsion she felt, as though she were dressing for Leo. But of course he wouldn't be there. Judy said that he never went to the club anymore.

A few minutes before seven, Gail went down to the lobby. Judy was waiting, looking quite chic in a green silk sheath.

"Hey, baby, you look great!" she told Gail.

"Am I too dressed up? I saw this dress in Naples and couldn't resist it."

"No, a lot of the women will be just as dressed up."

"Well, it's fun once in a while."

"By the way, Gail, I saw you driving off with Leo Shane the other day. What gives?"

"Nothing really. He was just going to Naples on business and thought I might like to go along. Actually, what he wanted was to talk me out of taking a position his uncle offered me."

"A job with Vince?" Judy's eyes widened.

"What on earth—oh, here come the guys! You'll have to tell me about it later."

Gail saw two young men coming through the lobby entrance. They were neatly dressed in slacks and sport jackets. Judy's fiance, Jeff Carnes, was a tall, bespectacled, pleasant-faced fellow with brown hair, brown eyes, and a boyish smile that made him look younger than his twenty-nine years.

The friend he had brought along for Gail was a shorter, stockier young man named Lyle Johnson, with sandy hair, blue eyes, fair skin that flushed easily, and attractive features. He seemed a bit on the shy side, and Gail liked him at once.

After the introductions and a bit of small talk, they drove off to the mainland in Jeff's little Toyota. The yacht club was about halfway up the coast between the island and Naples. Situated in a sheltered inlet, it had a large boat basin where members could rent slips for their boats. The clubhouse itself had a wide flagstone terrace at the edge of the water. The grounds were beautifully landscaped with many palms and flowering shrubs, while the interior was tastefully decorated.

The dining room had sliding glass doors opening onto the terrace where more tables had been set up. Next to the dining room, also opening onto the terrace, was a ballroom where a little combo was playing. Along one wall of the dining room was a long table with a lavish buffet where guests were already filling their plates. Opening off the dining room was a bar, also crowded.

Judy and Jeff seemed to know everybody, and there were many introductions as the two couples

made their way across the room. The majority of
guests were older people, but there was a smat-
tering of younger ones as well. It was a pleasant,
happy gathering, and Gail was glad she had
come.

Lyle proved to be a pleasant companion with a
nice sense of humor. After a round of drinks, and
some animated conversation in the bar, they
managed to work their way up to the buffet table
and filled their plates.

"Let's eat on the terrace," Judy suggested. "It's
nicer to sit by the water—if there are any tables
left."

Luckily, they found an empty table next to the
railing. The moon was up, trailing a path of
silver across the sea. Gail sighed. It was all so
romantic, but unfortunately she was with the
wrong man.

After they had eaten, they went into the
ballroom to dance. The combo was playing nos-
talgic music, some of it going as far back as the
thirties. Everyone danced in the old-fashioned
way, holding each other closely. A pleasant arrangement, Gail thought, and wasn't that what
dancing was for, really?

Lyle and Gail danced well together. He smelled
of some tangy shaving lotion, and his eyes were
admiring, his smile eager. By one of those coinci-
dences so curiously common in Florida, they
found that his hometown was only a hundred
miles or so from her own.

Gail danced with Jeff a few times and some of
the other men she had been introduced to, but
mostly, of course, with Lyle.

It must have been around ten-thirty when
Judy and Jeff danced by, close enough to touch,

and Judy murmured: "Hey, Gail, will wonders never cease! Look who just came in!"

Gail looked toward the entrance and could hardly restrain a little gasp. Leo was standing there, looking around with a smile, devastatingly attractive in a white linen suit, his pale hair gleaming under the lights. Beside him, clinging to his arm, was the most beautiful young woman Gail had ever seen: large green eyes, a mass of reddish-gold hair falling nearly to her slender waist, and exquisitely dainty features. She was wearing a white chiffon dress with a gold chain belt, and another gold chain glittered around her neck.

"The Lord and Lady Shane—in person!" Judy murmured. "When I count three, let's all curtsy!"

"Who is she?" Gail gasped.

"Vince's stepdaughter, I imagine. I wonder what she's doing here."

So that was the girl Leo had been in love with once, Gail thought in dismay. Or probably still was—how could any man stop loving a woman like that?

Then Leo's eyes met Gail's and, without realizing what she was doing, she moved away from Lyle and stood there staring at Leo as though mesmerized. The young woman murmured something to him and walked off toward the bar.

Leo walked slowly toward Gail and, without a word, she went into his arms and they danced away, leaving Lyle gazing after them with a surprised look on his face. The combo was playing the softly romantic "I'll See You Again," and Gail felt as though she were moving in a dream. Leo was much taller than she, and her head only came to his heart. She could hear it beating as she put her cheek against his chest and closed her eyes; she felt as though she had come home.

Leo moved with his natural grace as he steered her outside to the terrace.

"I thought you never came here," she murmured.

"The local grapevine again? True, I don't really care for these affairs, but this time there was a reason. Uncle's stepdaughter, Elizabeth, just arrived from the West Coast and there was someone she wanted to see. We were told that he was here, so she insisted on my bringing her."

Gail looked over toward the bar and saw Elizabeth standing near the entrance, talking with some agitation to a tall, good-looking man with smooth dark hair and rather hawklike features.

"Jay Baronelli," Leo said, "a lawyer. We've known him a long time, and Elizabeth wants him to help her. She always goes to him when she's in any sort of trouble."

"Is she in trouble now?" Gail asked.

"She thinks so. I'm not sure how serious it is— she has always been one to exaggerate things."

Leo did not say what the trouble was, but a wave of misery swept over Gail. If Elizabeth had left her husband and come back to the island. . . .

The lawyer and Elizabeth were on the terrace now and Gail could no longer see Elizabeth. When the combo stopped playing, Leo took Gail's hand, drawing her toward the steps that led down to the lawn.

"Gail, I want to talk to you for a few minutes —privately. Do you mind?"

She went with him along a flagstone walk leading to a little gazebo overlooking the Gulf.

"A beautiful night," Leo commented, "but getting a little cool. Do you think you need a wrap?"

She laughed. "Good heavens, when I left home I was wearing a heavy winter coat. This is summer weather to me. No, I'm fine."

He leaned against a pillar and looked down at her. "Is that the dress you bought in Naples?"

"Yes, do you like it?" Gail asked.

"I like you in it. You're looking very lovely tonight, Gail."

"Thank you. And I suppose all this is a prelude to another lecture on staying away from your uncle."

Leo laughed. "He's worried, you know, because you haven't been down to meet him on the beach the last few days. Is it because you took my warning seriously, or because you are thinking over his offer?"

"You certainly didn't succeed in scaring me off, and, yes, I am thinking it over. I thought I should stay away until I made up my mind."

"And have you made it up?" Leo asked.

"Just about. I think now I *will* accept it."

"Even though you must realize you might find yourself stranded and jobless in a few months?"

"I thought you said it would only take him a few weeks to get bored."

"With the memoirs—not with you. That would take a little longer."

Her face paled with anger and one hand went to her cheek, as though she had been struck. "That—that's a contemptible thing to say!" Gail cried and turned to leave.

"Gail!" He caught her wrist in his large, strong hand and pulled her back.

Caught off balance, she fell against him, and something swept through her, powerful as the wind. He slipped his arms around her, and his mouth came down on hers with angry, reluctant passion.

She knew she should break away, but the feel of his arms and the touch of his lips were too much for her. She could feel herself dissolving, melting, as she eagerly returned his kiss.

But then he released her, saying harshly: "Stay away from Samburan, Gail. It's no good for you."

She fled back to the safety of the lighted clubhouse and her waiting friends. At the door she caught her breath and paused, trying to calm herself, to look as though nothing had happened.

After counting slowly to ten, Gail walked across the room to where Lyle was standing, talking to Jeff and Judy.

Judy gave her a quick, searching glance, then said: "So there you are. We were just going to have another drink. How about it?"

"I could use one," Gail told her a bit grimly.

They went into the crowded bar.

"When you went off with Leo, we thought maybe we'd lost you for good," Judy said.

"Don't be silly. Leo just wanted to—to tell me something."

They carried their drinks out to the terrace.

"What happened to Elizabeth?" Gail asked Judy.

"Oh, she and Jay took off somewhere. I guess they had things to talk over. He's another one that was pretty far gone on her at one time."

"Is she very well known?" Gail asked. "As an actress, I mean. I've never seen her."

"She never had anything but bit parts, I guess."

"I've seen her," Lyle said. "On TV. She usually gets murdered or something in the first scene. She's very good at screaming."

"She's very beautiful," Gail commented.

"More so in person than on the screen," Lyle told her. "For some reason, she doesn't photograph too well. Other actresses are just the opposite. They don't look so great in person, but they photograph like a dream."

"It's the bone structure," Jeff murmured, sipping his drink.

"Did you say she married a director?" Gail asked.

Judy said, "Yeah. Some Hungarian, I think. Big guy with red hair. Wild temper and all that sort of thing. Maybe he beats her. Did you notice any bruises?"

"She looked great to me," Lyle said. "Didn't they have a child?"

"Yes, a little girl. She'd be about six by now. Did Leo say anything to you about what Elizabeth was doing here?" Judy asked Gail.

"No, only that she was in some sort of trouble and wanted to talk to Jay Baronelli."

By the time they had finished their drinks, Gail had fully regained her composure, but somehow the fun had gone out of the evening for her. Leo and the lovely Elizabeth never appeared again in the clubhouse, and Gail was glad to leave by midnight.

During the drive home, she could think of nothing but Leo and the feel of his arms around her—that devastating kiss. Was she going to accept Vince's offer, or should she follow Leo's advice and stay away from the Shanes?

They first drove to the apartment house where

the two young men lived, just outside Naples, so Lyle could get his car to take Gail home.

"You don't mind if we split up, do you?" Judy asked. "I'm going up to Jeff's for a while."

"No, that's okay." Gail and Lyle changed over to his car, and they headed back to the island.

She tried to respond to Lyle's lighthearted chatter about upstate New York and various other topics. But Gail's heart wasn't really in it, and she was relieved when they finally pulled up to the Sand Dollar. Lyle walked her to the elevators and gave her a rather quizzical smile.

"I know you don't want to ask me up," he said, "so I'll just say goodnight here."

"I'm sorry, Lyle," Gail replied. "I know I've been a drag tonight, but really I did have a nice time, and I like you very much. Thank you for taking me."

"I like you, too, Gail. I'd like to see you again, but I don't think I've got much of a chance, have I? Not with Leo Shane in residence."

"He hardly knows I exist, except as an annoyance," she told him. "Why don't you call me next week? Maybe we could get together again."

"I'd like that. Okay, I will. Goodnight, Gail." He kissed her lightly on the cheek and went away.

Gail stepped into the elevator and pushed the button. If it had been Leo who brought her home, she thought, she would certainly have asked him up. Yes, he was the one who was dangerous to her—not poor old Vince. A tide of reckless emotion swept over her, and she knew now that she was going to accept Vince's offer for sure. It was the only chance she had to stay close to Leo—at least for a little while.

CHAPTER SIX

Gail slept until nearly ten, then got up to fix some toast and coffee. She was just carrying it out to the balcony when the telephone rang. It was Vince. He sounded agitated. "I want to see you. This place is a madhouse—I've got to get out for a while. Harry is going to take me for a drive. Will you go with me?"

"Why, I suppose I could, Vince, but I'm not dressed yet, and I was just about to have breakfast."

"Say in about an hour?"

"All right. I'll be in the lobby."

Gail hung up and went back to her breakfast. It was a beautiful morning, as most mornings seemed to be in Florida. The waters of the Gulf were aquamarine near the shore and a deeper blue farther out. A crisp breeze was blowing. The beach below was crowded with gulls, some darting down toward a man who was tossing out bread crumbs. Quite a few small boats were out. What you would probably call Sunday sailors, Gail supposed. It would be fun to have a boat if you lived here. She thought about the cruiser she had seen moored at Samburan and wondered if Leo took it out very often.

When Gail had eaten and washed up the few dishes, she put on a pair of white slacks and a striped jersey, picked up her purse, and went downstairs. Judy wasn't in the office. She probably had the day off, Gail reflected. Her uncle was there instead. He was a widower and, although she hadn't talked to him very often, he seemed a pleasant man.

She was surprised when Harry pulled up at the entrance in the smaller car, as she had been expecting the Mercedes. After all, wasn't that Vince's car? Harry opened the car door for Gail and she climbed in beside Vince, who looked quite agitated.

"I'm glad you could come, Gail," he said. He was wearing a gray suit of some thin, tropical material and carried a silver-headed cane. His white hair was neatly combed and he really looked quite dapper, except for his fretful expression.

"What's the matter?" she asked as they drove off.

"I suppose you know that my stepdaughter is here," he replied. "Leo said he saw you at the club last night. Well, I'm supposed to be here for complete rest and quiet. But then Liz has to show up, carrying on about some big fight she had with

her husband, and that kid screaming bloody
murder half the night—"

"She has her little girl with her?" Gail interrupted.

"Yes, of course. That's the main reason she's
here—because she's afraid that her husband—
Laszlo Nagi—is going to try to take the kid away
from her and drag her off to Italy where he's
going to make a movie. They're getting a divorce.
It's a big mess, and I don't see why she has to
involve me!" He sounded like a petulant child.

"Maybe she has no one else to go to for help,"
Gail suggested gently.

"Oh, it wasn't me she came to—it was Leo, of
course, and that lawyer friend of hers. They were
both in love with her when she married Laszlo.
She even took my Mercedes this morning without
asking and went off to meet Jay somewhere! A
man can't have any peace in his own home!"

"Is the little girl really such a bother?" Gail
asked. "What's she like?"

"Her name's Elfrida. They call her Elfie. She
has a terrible temper, just like her father's. She
even looks like him, unfortunately. Spoiled rotten, of course."

Gail was beginning to feel very sorry for the
child. "Well, I'm sure this is very upsetting for
you," she said soothingly, "but it really isn't your
problem. And Elizabeth will no doubt get things
settled with her husband before long."

"I daresay. But I didn't get you here to talk
about them. I had to get away from the house and
that screaming kid for a while. I'm beginning to
feel like a prisoner—never a moment alone,
someone breathing down my neck all the time."

Vince glared at Harry's back. "And now there's two of them to plot against me. They don't expect me to live very long, you know, and they're going to make darn sure I don't marry again.

"Don't you see, Gail? I'm lonely and bored, and I need something to live for. Help me, my dear. Work with me on my memoirs. It's just what I need to take my mind off things." There were actually tears in his eyes as he reached out to take her hand.

Gail's tender heart was deeply moved, even though something inside her warned her that Leo was right—she really shouldn't get involved with the Shanes. Yet she wanted to help Vince—and she ached with the longing to stay near Leo, even if it was just for a little while.

"Well," she said slowly, "perhaps I could give it a try."

Vince's face lit up with excitement. "Splendid! Splendid, my dear. Later we'll go back to Samburan and I'll show you all the material I have for the memoirs. I've been trying to organize it a bit the last few days. But now we'll just drive up the coast for a while and have lunch somewhere. Perhaps things will have quieted down at home by then."

They reached the highway and Harry turned north toward Naples. They didn't stop in town, however, but went on to a beach resort farther up where they had lunch on a terrace overlooking the Gulf. Vince petulantly ordered Harry to take a seat at another table some distance from theirs.

"I see enough of your ugly face at home," he complained. "Let me enjoy at least one meal with only a pretty girl to look at."

Harry shrugged. "Okay, Vince," he said, "but if you try to sneak in a drink, I'm taking you out of here."

"Oh, go away!" Vince snarled. When Harry complied, Vince turned to Gail with a mock gesture of despair. "You see? What did I tell you? A prisoner, that's what I am. They won't even let me have a glass of wine."

"They're only trying to take care of you," she told him. "If you're recovering from a heart attack, you really shouldn't drink, I suppose. If Harry's your nurse, he must have had orders from your doctor. Really, Vince, you should be grateful that they care about you."

Gail was puzzled about the relationship between Vince and Harry. She had never known a patient-nurse relationship quite like theirs.

Vince shrugged and picked up a menu. "Well, if you'd like to order a drink, Gail, feel free. I don't mind."

"I never drink this early in the day. Alcohol makes me sleepy."

Then Vince entertained her with some stories about Paris.

But after their food arrived, he suddenly said: "I made a will last year leaving everything to Leo, except for a trust fund for Elizabeth. After all, I did adopt her, so I suppose I owe her something. Her own father died some time ago and left nothing at all. Leo, of course, should have Samburan because he's the only Shane left. Maybe if Elizabeth divorces Laszlo, she'll marry Leo after all, so she'll be well taken care of."

Gail felt a lump harden in her throat. "Do you think Leo still cares for her?" she asked.

"Who knows? He's a strange one. Never did understand him. Can't see why he's content to lead the life he does."

"What is his life exactly up in Sweden?" Gail picked up her fork and began eating her scallops although somehow she'd lost her appetite.

"As far as I can see, he's nothing but a glorified farmer. Oh, they have tenant farmers who do the actual work, but he supervises everything. Sort of a lord of the manor deal—you know what I mean."

Gail wasn't sure that she did. "What crops do they raise?" she asked.

"Oh, heavens, how should I know!" Vince looked annoyed. He obviously was getting bored with the conversation. "I never could stand farms. I never go there unless I have to, although I'm very fond of Leo's mother. Lovely woman."

They finished their lunch and then Vince decided it was time to return to Samburan.

"Harry will make me take a rest, of course," he told Gail, "but you can look over the material I've laid out for you. Get an idea of how you want to handle it. I know nothing whatsoever about the construction of a book, you know."

"All right, Vince," she agreed.

She wondered if Leo would be there—and how would he react to her presence after his dramatic exit line at the yacht club?

They drove back to the island. When they walked into the living room, Leo and a very tiny girl were sitting at the piano playing a duet. On the floor beside them sat an enormous brown teddy bear with a sad, battered face and a missing ear. The child looked up at them with a don't-bother-me-now expression and went on to finish the selection.

Gail applauded when Leo rose from the bench. "Very good! I didn't realize you were so talented."

He gave her a wry little smile and the child regarded her with big, solemn eyes. "I'm giving him lessons," she explained.

She was very pale, with flaming red hair braided into tight pigtails, a thin, freckled face, a wide mouth with one front tooth missing, and enormous green eyes. She was wearing shorts and a T-shirt, both rather soiled. She was not at all what Gail had expected; she looked like a pitiful little waif rather than the spoiled child of wealthy Hollywood parents.

"Elfie, this is Gail Durand," Leo told her. "Gail, this is Elfie."

The child made a little curtsying movement with her legs and bobbed her head. "I'm pleased to meet you, Miss Durand," she said primly.

"And who is that?" Gail nodded at the bear.

"That is Mr. Jones. He's my friend."

"How do you do, Mr. Jones," Gail said gravely to the creature that was nearly as big as the child.

"Well, I'm glad you've decided to stop screaming, at least," Vince told Elfie rather pettishly.

Elfie gave him an unfriendly glance. "I was screaming at Mommy," she said coldly. "But she isn't here now, so it wouldn't be very sensible to go on with it, would it?" She sounded much more like twenty than six.

Vince suddenly looked very tired and Gail noticed that his hands were shaking. "I think," he said, "that I will have to take a little rest before we look over my notes, Gail. You will excuse me, won't you? This has been a trying day. Leo can show you where the stuff is if you want to go over it by yourself."

"Of course," she replied.

Harry was there at once, taking Vince by the arm, leading him toward his room. "I told you it would be too much for you to go for such a long ride in the car," he said as they went out.

"Why don't we go for a walk on the beach?" Elfie suggested eagerly. "In our bare feet."

"Oh, certainly in our bare feet," Leo said, promptly kicking off his sandals. "How else does one walk on a beach? But perhaps Miss Durand would prefer to go over your grandfather's papers."

"He's not my grandfather," Elfie objected. "Mommy says we're not really related at all, and I'm glad. You'd rather walk on the beach than look at his old papers, wouldn't you, Miss Durand?"

"Much rather," Gail admitted.

"Mr. Jones," Elfie said with a loving pat, "you will have to stay here. It isn't good for you to get your paws sandy." She looked at Gail. "Well, Miss Durand, aren't you going to take your shoes off?"

Gail looked uncertainly at Leo. "Are you sure you want me to go along?"

"Of course," Elfie told her. "It wouldn't be polite not to invite you."

Gail slipped off her shoes and they went down to the cove, with Elfie between them, holding a hand of each. She never stopped talking.

"I was screaming at Mommy," she explained to Gail, "because I want to go to Italy with Daddy, and she won't go. I always enjoy going on location

with him because we meet such interesting people, and they make a fuss over me. Once I got to
ride in a real submarine. Mommy never listens to
me. She isn't very sensible, I'm afraid. If she were
sensible, she would do what Daddy tells her.
Don't you think it would be more sensible for her
to go to Italy than to stay in Hollywood and make
dumb commercials, Miss Durand?"

"More fun, anyway," Gail agreed. "But maybe
she likes making commercials, and she does have
her own career to consider, doesn't she?" It
seemed natural to talk to Elfie as though she
were adult. After all, that was how the little girl
talked.

"Some career!" Elfie scoffed. "Daddy says that
while she's adorable, she can't act her way out of
a barrel of monkeys! Daddy talks funny sometimes. He's Hungarian, you know. That's why he
won't put her in his films, which makes her as
mad as a wet hornet!"

"A wet hornet?" Gail mused.

"Daddy says. He thinks she ought to stay home
and have lots and lots of babies."

"Do you agree with him?"

Elfie looked thoughtful. "Well, no. Not about
all the babies. I'd rather be an only child. But I do
want to go to Italy."

They had reached the open beach where the
sandpipers were disporting. With a cry of delight,
Elfie let go of their hands and went running after
them. Leo and Gail followed more slowly.

"What a wonderful child," Gail commented.

"I think so, but some people consider her a
brat—especially Uncle."

"She's not a brat at all!" Gail said indignantly.
"No doubt she's had an unconventional upbring-

ing and has associated mainly with adults, but she is certainly very intelligent."

"Yes, she's quite precocious," Leo agreed.

He sounded rather wistful and Gail wondered if he regretted the fact that Elizabeth had not married him and that Elfie was not his child.

"Do you think her parents are really on the verge of a divorce?" she asked cautiously.

Leo shrugged. "It certainly looks that way at the moment, but this sort of thing happens at regular intervals. And so far they've always gone back together. What can you expect when two temperamental redheads get married?" He gave her a searching look. "So you came here today to go over Uncle's papers with him? Then I assume you're seriously considering going to work for him."

"I told him I would," she said defiantly. "Except for vague warnings, you haven't given me any real reasons why I shouldn't."

"You're not afraid of being out of a job in a short time?"

"I told you I was thinking of making a break anyway. I'm in a rut at home. I want to get a job on one of the big papers somewhere. Of course, the job with Vince would be temporary, but it's a change, I like it here, and I can be thinking over what I really want to do."

He sighed. "All right, Gail. I'm not going to fight you on this any longer. If you're sure this is what you want, go ahead. It will probably be good for him to get his mind off his illness for a while."

"I'm sure it will."

"About last night—at the club"—he looked suddenly uncomfortable—"I'm sorry about the way I behaved, Gail. Will you forgive me and be friends?"

She stopped and looked up at him. He seemed sincere, but what was he really thinking behind those compelling blue-green eyes? Was he still afraid that she wanted to marry Vince?

"Why not?" she said.

"Good!" Leo gave her a smile that made her toes curl and held out his hand. "A truce!"

Gail put her hand into his, feeling the excitement of his touch, wondering what she was getting herself into, and not really caring as long as it meant she would go on seeing Leo. "A truce," she agreed.

Elfie came running back to them, her pale freckled face glowing.

"Were you talking about me?" she demanded.

"Of course not, you vain creature," Leo retorted. "We were talking about your grandfather. Miss Durand is going to work for him and help him write a book."

Elfie wrinkled her little snub nose. "He's not my grandfather. One of my real grandfathers lived in Hungary, but he's dead. And the other one died before I was born, so I'm stuck with Vince. But I won't call him Grandpa. He hates it when I do, anyway. I wish I had a nice friendly one, like the ones in books, who would hold me on his knees and tell me stories about the good old days." She sounded wistful.

"Well, you've got me, anyway," Leo said. "I tell you stories."

"Yes, and I love you, but you're too young to be a grandpa. You're just sort of a cousin, aren't you?"

"Something like that."

"You're not Mommy's real cousin, though. You could marry her if you wanted to. Would you like me to be your little girl?"

"I'd love that, darling, but your father loves you, too, and I'm sure he wouldn't want you to live with anyone else."

She sighed. "I know. I do love him best, but he's not home very much. I wish adults weren't so unreliable."

"We do seem to excel in creating problems for ourselves," Leo admitted wryly.

"Maybe I could live with you and your mommy in Sweden," Elfie suggested, "and Daddy could come to see me when he's in Europe. Do you know, Miss Durand, they live in a big house like a castle and have horses and dogs and five cats? I think that would be a very sensible arrangement."

To Elfie, Gail mused, being sensible was the ultimate achievement for a human being of any age. Well, she herself was probably not being very sensible in throwing up her job to work for Vince—but she still intended to do it!

CHAPTER SEVEN

When Gail, Leo, and Elfie got back to the house, Elizabeth was there, pacing up and down the living room, her lovely hair in disarray, her eyes burning with some emotion Gail could not identify. Elizabeth was complaining to Mary Forbes about the lack of anything to drink in the house. When she saw Leo, she ran and threw her arms around him.

"Oh, darling, I'm so glad you're here! I just had a phone call from Jimmy—"

"Jimmy?"

"My agent, you know that! He said that Laszlo is on his way to Italy and that he plans to stop off here first to get Elfie! He's determined to take her with him, even if I won't go. He thinks I don't look after her properly! As if he'd have time for

her himself when he's working—Leo, what
should I do? Call the police?"

Elfie let out a howl. "I don't want them to ar-
rest Daddy!"

"Now, now," Leo said soothingly, "nobody is
going to be arrested. I'm sure that Laszlo will listen to reason."

"Laszlo never listens to reason!" Elizabeth
wailed. "You know how Hungarians are. Jimmy
says he's as mad as a—a—"

"Wet hornet?" Gail suggested from the couch,
where she had seated herself to watch this interesting little scene.

Elizabeth gave her an angry glare, then turned
back to Leo. "He'll probably be here tomorrow
some time. Maybe you could take Elfie and go
someplace where he can't find you. Then I'll get
Jay to come over and talk to Laszlo. When he
realizes Elfie isn't here, maybe he'll give up and
go on to Italy. He can't afford to delay too long—
he should have been there last week, but he was
trying to talk me into going with him."

"So was I," Elfie put in. "It's really the only
sensible thing to do, Mommy."

Elizabeth turned her glare on the child.
"Shouldn't you be taking a nap or something?"
she demanded.

"Yes, but Leo doesn't make me. We agreed that
I'm not a baby anymore."

"You were never a baby!" Elizabeth said. "But
go up and try, anyway. I've got to talk to Leo.
Privately." She gave Gail another angry glance.

"Excuse me," Leo said, "I should have introduced you. Gail, this is Elizabeth Nagi. Liz, Gail
Durand."

"How do you do, Mrs. Nagi," Gail murmured

and rose from the couch. "Well, I think I'd better run along now." She turned to Leo. "Please tell Vince I'll come over tomorrow and go through his papers with him. Somehow this doesn't seem to be the right time for it."

"All right, I'll tell him," Leo said, looking rather harried.

Elfie took Mr. Jones by his one remaining ear and walked slowly out of the room, followed by Gail.

In the hall the child looked at her solemnly and said: "We're being evicted."

"That's all right, Elfie. I'll see you tomorrow, I suppose."

"Unless Leo drags me off somewhere to hide from Daddy. I don't think that's very sensible myself." She went up the stairs, Mr. Jones bumping along behind.

When Gail reached the front door, Harry appeared. "Want me to drive you home?" he asked.

She looked at him. Something about the man always made her uncomfortable. "No, thanks. I'd rather walk."

He shrugged. "Suit yourself."

Back at the Sand Dollar, as Gail was walking through the lobby, Judy popped out of her little cubicle.

"Hey, Gail! I've been wanting to talk to you. It's coffee-break time, so come on and I'll buy you a cup."

When they were seated in the coffee shop and the waitress had brought them their cups, Judy said: "You made a terrific impression on Lyle last night. Jeff told me so this morning when he called. Lyle's dying to ask you for another date, but he thinks you've got a yen for Leo Shane."

"I liked Lyle," Gail replied. "I wouldn't mind going out with him again."

"What was it you were starting to tell me last night about going to work for Vince Shane? Surely you jest!"

"He wants to write his memoirs, and he asked me to work on them with him. I told him I would."

Judy sighed, lit a cigarette, and blew smoke at the ceiling. "I'm sure they'd be pretty hot stuff—but, my heavens, Gail—"

"I know, I know!" Gail headed her off quickly. "I've already heard all the arguments from Leo. But don't you see, Judy, even if it doesn't last, I can save some money and think about getting a job on a big newspaper when this is over. And if this all falls apart, I can just go home and—"

"Baby, it's not the job that worries me," Judy told her. "And Vince is probably harmless by now. But Leo—are you sure you know what you're doing?"

"No, I'm not sure of anything, but I still intend to give it a try. I'm certainly not getting anywhere stuck back in that little town."

"Well, lots of luck, baby. I've a feeling you're going to need it. Were you over at Samburan today? Did you see Elizabeth?"

Gail told her what had happened. "I really feel sorry for little Elfie," she concluded. "They're giving her a rough time."

"Oh, I don't know," Judy mused. "I've a feeling she rather enjoys it. When you start working for Vince, are you going to move over there?"

"Not until my time is up here," Gail told her. "Then I guess I'll have to. I don't think I could afford to rent anything on the island. We've never discussed it, but I imagine Vince is taking that for granted."

"I wonder how long Elizabeth will hang around?"

"Not very long, I'm sure. She has to go back to Hollywood and make some commercials."

"And I've got to get back to the office and finish my work." Judy stood up. "Things sure have livened up since you got here, Gail. It's as good as a TV show any day. Be seeing you."

The next morning Gail went back to Samburan, a little uncertain about what she might walk into this time.

When Mary let Gail in, she said:

"Mr. Vince is a bit under the weather today, Miss Durand, and that Harry's keeping him in bed. But I think Mr. Leo wants to see you about something. Go on into the living room."

Leo was playing cards with Elfie on the coffee table. As Gail walked in, Elfie threw her cards down with a triumphant cry of "Gin!"

Leo got to his feet. "Thank heaven you're here, Gail! This child is clobbering me."

Elfie ran over to her and said excitedly, "Guess what, Miss Durand! We're going off in the cruiser, just you and me and Leo! Won't that be fun?"

"Now, Elfie," Leo protested, "you know Miss Durand hasn't agreed to go yet."

"But you will, won't you, Miss Durand?" Elfie looked up with pleading green eyes.

Gail sat down on the couch. "It would be nice if someone would tell me what this is all about," she said.

"They want to hide me from Daddy!" Elfie cried. "I didn't want to go at first—it was just going to be Leo and me. And I explained to them that men didn't understand how to look after little girls, so Mommy said we could take you along."

"Elfie," Leo said, "suppose you run out to the kitchen and see if Mary has any cookies. Okay?"

Elfie gave him an annoyed glance. "If you want to talk to her alone, just say so, Leo. Don't give me that cookie routine. I'm going up and pack my bag. And don't forget—you owe me thirty dollars."

Leo watched her go with a rueful smile. "Formidable!" he murmured.

"Leo, are you really teaching that child to gamble?" Gail demanded.

"Who—me? Teach HER? She picked that up on the sets with her mother in Hollywood. But don't worry—we're only using play money. How about it, Gail? Would you be willing to go for a little trip in the cruiser—maybe stay out overnight? The crisis will probably be over by then."

Gail didn't know what to say. "Well, I—it's rather—"

"It would help us over an awkward confrontation with Laszlo, and Vince isn't up to working with you today, anyway. You know it really isn't good for Elfie to be around when her parents have one of their screaming sessions."

Gail was weakening. "Is Vince very ill?" she asked.

"Nothing serious. Just tired. He'll be all right by tomorrow. Will you go, Gail? Harry can run you home to get whatever you'll need, and I'll get the boat ready. We'll just run down among the islands a bit—we've done it many times. You'll like it down there."

"Where is Elizabeth now?" she asked.

"Sleeping. She didn't get much sleep last night worrying about Laszlo, I suppose."

"Well—all right, Leo. I suppose it will be all right."

When Gail came downstairs with her small canvas flight bag, she stopped at the office.

"Judy," she said, "I just wanted to let you know that I'll be away overnight, in case anything comes up. I'm going for a little cruise in the Shanes' boat."

Judy stared at her blankly. "Who with?" she demanded. "Not Leo, I hope!"

"Well, not alone. It's rather complicated. We're taking Elfie away for a while because her father is coming and Elizabeth is afraid he might try to take her—Elfie, that is—to Rome with him."

Judy put up her hands in a gesture of surrender. "Never mind! Say no more. Just go away and do your thing and tell me about it when you get back. Okay?"

"Okay," Gail said.

She went out to Harry and the waiting car.

At the Shane house, Elfie was waiting for Gail on the back veranda with her flight bag and Mr. Jones.

"Leo's down at the boat," she said. "He told me to bring you down when you came. Won't it be fun, Miss Durand?"

"I think so," Gail agreed.

They went across the lawn to the dock where the cruiser was moored. Gail didn't know much about boats, but she judged it to be about a thirty-footer, an old model, no flying bridge, just a pleasant-looking little craft. Leo was carrying some boxes down to the cabin.

"Welcome aboard," he said. "Everything's ready. We'll take off right away."

In a short time Gail found herself sitting on the aft deck between Elfie and Mr. Jones, while Leo steered the craft smoothly out of the bay into the more open waters to the south.

"Mrs. Forbes packed us lots of food, so we won't have to cook," Elfie told Gail. "Isn't this fun?"

"Terrific!" Gail agreed, wondering ruefully how she had managed to get so deeply involved with the Shanes in such a short period of time.

But here she was, heading into unknown waters, both literally and figuratively. She looked over to where Leo was standing at the helm. He had taken off his shirt and was wearing only white trunks, his tanned body and golden hair gleaming in the sunshine. He seemed even more appealing than a young Robert Redford. How would she stand it?

Following her gaze, Elfie remarked: "He's very handsome, isn't he?"

"Yes, he is," Gail agreed.

"I love him best, next to Mommy and Daddy, of course. Maybe a little bit better than Mommy because he's more sensible. Would you like me to show you what's downstairs? I mean, below. That's what you say on boats. Below. And the bathroom is called a head. Isn't that silly?"

"Very." Gail nodded.

They went down the short ladder. There was a tiny galley, a head, a dinette in the main cabin that could be folded down into a bed, and a very small stateroom with two bunks, one above the other.

"We'll sleep in here, I guess," Elfie said. "Leo will probably sleep in the lounge, or whatever you call it. Only, sometimes he goes up on deck. He likes to sleep under the stars. So do I, but they're afraid I'll fall overboard. Sometimes I walk in my sleep."

"Have you been on many cruises?" Gail asked.

"No, just a few times when we come here to visit in the winter. I wished we lived here instead of California. It's much nicer. The water is too rough and cold there, and I can never go swimming. I can swim here. Don't you think Florida is nice, Miss Durand?"

"Very nice. You can call me Gail if you want to."

"Well, Daddy doesn't like me to call adults by their first names—it isn't considered respectful in Europe."

"What about Leo?"

"That's different. He's my cousin. Only, when Daddy's here, I'm supposed to call him Cousin Leo. Maybe it would be all right if I called you Miss Gail."

"Okay, Elfie. I'd like that."

They went back on deck. Out in the open water, the swells rolled the little boat. But before Gail had a chance to get squeamish, they were in the shelter of a group of small islands. Soon Leo cruised in close to one with a small beach among some mangroves, then cast anchor. They waded ashore, Leo carrying the picnic hamper. It was a beautiful, secluded spot, with white sand.

They had all put on their bathing suits before going ashore, so now they had a swim in the cool water. Elfie had never really learned to swim properly. She splashed around a lot until Leo tried to give her a few pointers. When they'd had enough of that, they went ashore and dried off a

bit, then ate their lunch. Gail thought she had
never tasted anything better than the cold fried
chicken, potato salad, and home-baked bread.

"It's so peaceful here," she remarked when she
could eat no more. "As though we were the only
people left in the world."

"I wish we were!" Elfie cried and ran off to ex-
plore.

The sun was very warm and Gail felt drowsy
after the swim and the big meal. Leo stretched
out on the big beach towel and she lay beside
him, suppressing an urge to touch his smooth
brown arm.

"Do you really live in a castle?" she murmured.

He smiled at her. "No, of course not, just an old
estate house. It's a beautiful area, near the
straits that separate Sweden from Denmark. We
swim there in the summer, where the wild swans
come down into the sea."

"It sounds like poetry," Gail said.

"Sweden is a very beautiful country. I wish I
could show it to you."

Elfie came back in a few minutes and curled up
between them. Soon they all drifted off to sleep.
Later they swam again. Then Leo moved the boat
farther down among the islands to a place he said
would give them better anchorage for the night.
These islands were a haven for birds, and Gail
was thrilled to see herons, pelicans, cormorants,
and others sharing the same rookeries.

"It's a true paradise down here," she observed.
"I had no idea Florida was like this."

"This is the real Florida," Leo told her. "Not
the Florida of Miami Beach and the overbuilt
coastlines and keys. Fortunately, this is all protected now, so you can get an idea of what it was

like here long ago, before the white men came
and spoiled it. Of course, it isn't all paradise. This
area can be ravaged by terrible storms. And in
the summer the mosquitoes can drive you crazy."

The island that Leo selected for their overnight
stay was tiny but well protected from the open
Gulf. It had a natural little cove where they took
a final swim. When it got dark, they built a small
fire on the sand and roasted hot dogs for their
supper. Then they sat by the dying fire and Leo
told them stories of the strange, fierce tribe of
Indians that had once lived there.

"They had quite a well-developed culture,
those Calusas," he said, "with an elaborate sys-
tem of mounds, courts, plazas, and canals in this
area."

"Were they burial mounds?" Gail asked.

"Some were. A lot of them were just kitchen
garbage dumps where they threw their oyster
shells and so on—like the mound Samburan is
built on. Later, when death became more of a rit-
ual, they made special burial mounds of shells on
these islands, and of rocks and sand on others
farther inland."

Next Leo spoke about the funeral rites, men-
tioning a bowl carved from the top of a human
skull.

Elfie was intrigued. "Hey, terrific!" she cried.
"I wish I had one of those to drink my milk out
of!"

"What a ghoulish little monster you are," Leo
said.

"They sound like a fascinating people," Gail
observed.

He kept talking about the Calusas until Elfie
fell asleep on the beach blanket. Then he carried

her back to the boat and Gail took her below to
help her wash off the sand and get into her pajamas.

"Do you want to sleep up or down?" Gail asked.

"Oh, up, please! I always do." Elfie scrambled
up the little ladder and cuddled down on the
upper bunk. "Please hand me Mr. Jones," she re-
quested. "He always stays with me when I sleep."

There was hardly room up there for both of
them, but Gail managed to stuff the teddy bear in
beside the child.

"Have you had him long?" she asked.

"Oh, yes. Ever since I was little."

"Who gave him to you?" Gail asked.

"I don't know. God, I guess. I woke up one
morning and there he was, standing by my bed.
Mr. Jones, I mean. Not God. We've been friends
ever since."

Gail reached up to kiss her. "Goodnight, darling. Sweet dreams."

"Goodnight, Miss Gail. Tell Leo to come down
and kiss me, too."

"Okay."

Gail left a dim night light burning and went
back on deck. Leo was sitting there smoking,
gazing at the stars.

"Elfie wants to kiss you goodnight," she said.

Apparently, he intended to sleep on deck because he had brought an air mattress up and in-
flated it. While he was gone, Gail sat on it and
gazed at the stars herself. They were so bright, so
peaceful.

Soon Leo was back. Gail felt his warmth and
exciting nearness as he dropped down beside her.

"Shall we swim again?" he asked. "This is the

best time—by starlight." They still had their
suits on.

"All right," she agreed.

They climbed down the ladder and dropped
into the water, which felt warmer at night. As
Gail slowly swam beside Leo, she felt curiously
disembodied, as though she were floating in some
magic liquid space where water and sky were one
and the stars were keeping them safe. As if sus-
pended in a dream, they swam into the silver
path of the moon. And Gail felt united with the
sea, with the night, with the moon and the stars
—with the vast, mysterious universe.

"We'd better not go too far," Leo warned her.
"You might get another cramp."

"I feel as though I could swim forever," Gail
murmured, but they turned back toward the
cruiser.

She was terribly conscious of him there beside
her. His arm touched hers, and a quiver ran
through her. Did Leo feel it, too?

He followed her up the ladder to the deck.
Then his arms went around her, and his mouth
came down on hers.

Gail clung to him, one hand in his hair, as he
gently kissed her temples, her throat, her eyes.
Then, as his lips met hers again, an unearthly
howl tore through the quiet night.

CHAPTER EIGHT

"It's Elfie!" Gail cried, breaking away from Leo's embrace and dashing down the inner ladder to the cabin.

She found the child sitting up in her bunk, clutching Mr. Jones to her breast, and letting out one howl after another.

Gail climbed up to the frightened child and put her arms around her. "Darling, what's the matter?"

"The Indians!" Elfie sobbed. "They were going to kill me and drink my blood out of the skull!"

So this was what Leo got for telling such gruesome stories at bedtime, Gail thought, rocking the child gently in her arms.

"It was only a dream, Elfie," she murmured. "It's all right now. I'm here and nothing can hurt you."

Leo stuck his head in the door. "What on earth's the matter?" he asked.

"Just a bad dream," Gail told him. "You shouldn't have told her those wild stories about the skulls."

"I'm sorry," he said contritely. "I didn't think."

"That's all right, Leo," Elfie told him and lay back on her pillow with a quivering sigh. "I guess it was mostly that I ate too much. I have a very delicate digestion, you know."

He remained uncertainly in the doorway. "Is there anything I can do?"

"No, I'll be all right now. But I'd like Gail to stay with me, if that's okay with you."

"Of course, sweetheart," Leo said, shutting the cabin door behind him.

Elfie heaved another sigh. "Boy, that was a real zinger!" she said.

"Do you have nightmares often?"

"No, only when I get upset or eat too much. It isn't that I don't like being here with you and Leo." Her sharp green eyes surveyed Gail curiously, taking in the damp hair, the wet suit. "You went swimming again," she said.

"Yes, just a quick dip in the moonlight."

"You'd better put on something dry. You might catch cold."

"I'm sure you're right," Gail said.

She quickly slipped out of her suit and into her pajamas. Then she sat on the cabin's only chair and began to brush her wet hair.

"Was Leo romancing you?" Elfie asked calmly.

Gail stared at her in blank dismay. What kind of a child was this? "What makes you think that?" was all she could say.

"Well, I thought he might. Mommy told him to."

Gail's body seemed to grow cold, as though encased in ice. "What do you mean, Elfie?"

"I heard them talking on the back porch last night. There's a balcony upstairs right over it, you know, and I sneaked out there after Mommy put me to bed. I like to lie on the couch out there and listen to the little frogs and night birds and all that stuff. Of course, they didn't know I could hear them. But I could.

"And Mommy asked him if you were one of Vince's girls. Well, Leo said not exactly, but you were going to help Vince write a book. Mommy said that was a crazy idea. With Vince one thing always led to another, and he—Leo—better break it up right now and dis—distract you from Vince, even if he had to act like he loved you himself. She said they couldn't afford another one—whatever that meant."

Gail stared at the child while the ice grew deeper. She felt as though she would never be warm again.

"What did Leo say to that?" she asked, barely able to move her lips in the Arctic cold.

"I don't know. Harry came out to ask Leo something, and I was getting cold, so I went back to bed. Is it fun to kiss and act all mushy, Miss Gail? I've seen them do it in films, of course, but that couldn't be real because it's too silly."

"You're too young to think about such things," Gail said, putting down the brush and crawling into her own bunk. "Go back to sleep. I'll be right here."

In a few minutes Elfie seemed to be asleep

again, but Gail lay staring sightlessly at the bunk over her head. She couldn't seem to stop shivering. Now she realized how childish she had been to allow her feelings for Leo Shane to get the better of her.

Why, she meant nothing to him. Nothing at all. She was just someone to be disposed of before she could get her hooks into Vince. Probably Leo was still in love with Elizabeth. Were those two planning to combine forces and marry when Elizabeth got rid of Laszlo? Then they could share Vince's fortune—if they could keep him from marrying again.

Now a hot tide of anger and shame rushed over Gail, melting the ice. No doubt Leo thought he had only to crook a finger and any woman would fall panting into his arms! As she had done! Oh, how gullible she had been! How could she have trusted him? He himself had warned her to keep away from the Shanes. Well, at least she had learned the truth in time to avoid complete disaster.

So much for love and romance, Gail thought bitterly. But now, what was she going to do? Forget the Shanes, go back where she came from? Words began to form in her mind for the speech she would make to Leo before she went. For quite a while she lay there planning exactly what she would say, words that would make him cringe with shame.

But would they? A man like him—a man without honor or decency—a man who would stop at nothing to keep a sick old man under his thumb in order to gain control of his fortune— would mere words mean anything to a man like that? Probably not. More than likely Leo would only laugh at her.

For instead of a heart he had a built-in calculator. Money was the only thing that meant anything to Leo Shane. If she really wanted to hurt him, the only way was to prevent him from ever seeing a penny of the Shane fortune. But there was no way she could do that. Yes, there was! There was a way, the only way. She could marry Vince Shane!

Leo and Elizabeth seemed convinced that Vince wanted to marry her. Gail herself was not all that certain of it, but she could pretend a romantic interest in Vince. She could make him propose to her. And she would do it—just to get back at Leo! She'd be doing Vince a favor, too. He was so bored, so unhappy about his virtual imprisonment at Samburan. She could "rescue" him from all that, take him away to his beloved France. Yes, that would do very nicely. She could just picture Leo and Elizabeth fuming with rage while she and Vince sailed off into the sunset! Perfect.

With that decided, Gail tried to fall asleep. She tossed and turned for a long, long time, however. When she finally did manage to close her eyes, she was plagued by troubled dreams.

Gail woke up early the next morning. At first she had no idea where she was. Then it all came flooding back to her, including the plan she'd made last night to go after Vince and marry him.

Of course, in the light of day, Gail realized she could never do that. She simply didn't have it in her. But there was something she could do. She could try to protect Vince from the greedy clutches of Leo and Elizabeth. She could try to free him from his prison and see that he led a life as normal as possible. Yes, she would do what she could for Vince. And the sooner Leo knew about it, the better.

Fortunately, Elfie was still sleeping, worn out by her disturbed night, so Gail slipped into her shorts and jersey, paid a quick visit to the head to try and erase some of the night's ravages, and then went out to face Leo.

He was sitting in the little dinette drinking coffee and looked up with a smile.

"Good morning! Want some coffee? It's fresh brewed."

She poured herself a cup and slid into the seat opposite him. "Good morning, Leo." Cool and crisp and no-nonsense.

He gave her a slightly quizzical look. "Elfie still asleep?"

"Yes, she is," Gail said.

"Poor little tyke. I guess I'm not very good with children. But she always liked—"

"You're fine with her," Gail interrupted. "I think it was the hot dogs, not the stories."

"Well, perhaps it's just as well we were interrupted." He gently put his hand on hers. "I don't want you to think—"

She pulled her hand away as though she had been burned. "Wait a minute, Leo. There's something I want to say before you go any farther. Last night was a mistake, that's all. It never should have happened and it will never happen again. I was just carried away by the romantic, tropical night. After all, I am human, you know.

But I haven't the slightest intention of getting involved with you in any way. Is that quite clear?"

Gone was the look of tenderness that had been in Leo's eyes a moment before. "I see," he said flatly. "You've decided to go for the bigger game after all."

"I'm going to work for Vince, if that's what you mean. And I'll try to give him the support and sympathy that seem so lacking in his life."

A flicker of pain and disillusionment crossed Leo's face. "And to think that I believed you were different from the others. That you—"

Elfie came trailing out in her pajamas, dragging Mr. Jones behind her. "I heard you talking," she said. "Is breakfast ready?"

"It will be in a minute." Leo got up and looked down at her with an anxious frown. "Are you all right this morning, darling?"

"I guess so." Elfie slid listlessly into the place he had vacated. "But I just might throw up if we hit any waves."

"Oh, good grief," he muttered. "That's all I need!"

"Maybe I'd better not eat much breakfast," she told him. "Just some milk and a piece of toast. Or maybe a croissant. You know, a Continental breakfast."

"Sorry," he said, "I'm fresh out of croissants. I'll make us some toast. How about you, Gail?"

"Just toast, thank you. I'm not very hungry either."

While they waited for Leo to make the toast, Elfie looked thoughtfully at Gail. "Did you and Leo have a fight?" she asked. "You both have that look in your eyes like Mommy and Daddy do when they've been fighting. Only, they usually yell. I didn't hear any yelling."

"No, we didn't have a fight," Gail said. "What would we have to fight about?"

"Oh, you could find something. People usually do. I don't see why, though. It always spoils the fun. It just isn't sensible. When I grow up and get married, I'm never going to fight at all. I'll just be happy, happy, happy all the time."

"Then you'd better learn to stop screaming every time you don't get your own way," Leo told her from the galley. "You'll never be happy if you do that."

Elfie nodded. "I guess you're right. But that's what Mommy does, and then Daddy screams right back. From now on, I'm going to practice not screaming."

"Good." Leo came over with a plate of toast and a glass of milk. "I'm sure your grandfather will be delighted to hear that."

"He's not my grandfather." Elfie took some toast and nibbled it halfheartedly.

Leo brought the coffeepot over and filled his and Gail's cups again. "You know," he said, "I think it might be best if we just go back to Samburan instead of going on south. The radio said something about a storm moving in by afternoon, and if Elfie's feeling squeamish..."

"I think that's a good idea," Gail agreed. The sooner this ill-fated voyage was over, the better.

"I guess so," Elfie said. "We can go back and see how Mommy's making out." She brightened. "Maybe Daddy will still be there! Maybe he'll take me to Italy!"

Gail cleaned up the few dishes while Leo got

the boat under way. Then Gail joined the other two on deck. If there was a storm coming, there was no sign of it yet. The sun was shining and the water was still and beautiful.

They reached Samburan before noon. While Leo secured the boat, Elfie and Gail walked up the path to the back veranda, carrying their bags and Mr. Jones. Elizabeth was sitting in a wicker rocker, reading a magazine, looking sleek and beautiful in white shorts and a tailored white blouse. Elfie ran to her, dropping Mr. Jones in her haste.

"We're back, Mommy! Did Daddy come?"

Elizabeth kissed her and smoothed back the disordered hair from the child's flushed face. "Hello, darling. Yes, Daddy was here, but he's gone now."

Her eyes went to Gail, who had paused at the top of the steps. Gail flushed with anger. Elizabeth was trying to determine whether she had been romanced, no doubt.

Elfie's lower lip quivered. "Was he very mad because I wasn't here?"

"Not really. He knew he couldn't very well take you without me. Did you enjoy the cruise, Miss Durand?"

"It's very lovely down among the islands," Gail replied stiffly.

Leo came up the path carrying the remains of the food in a picnic hamper.

"How did it go?" he asked Elizabeth.

"All right. Laszlo came and we talked everything over. He'd calmed down a lot. We agreed that I'd go home and do the commercials and let Elfie finish the school year. I have her in a private school now, you know, and it's very good.

Then in May, if the film isn't finished, we can both go to Italy to stay with Laszlo for the summer."

"And you aren't going to divorce him?" Elfie demanded.

"No, darling, you know that was just talk."

"Hooray!" Elfie pranced around the porch. "And maybe when the film's done, we can all go up and stay with Leo in his castle for a while!"

"Maybe." Elizabeth flashed a look at Leo that Gail could not interpret. "We'll see."

"Daddy would say, 'We shouldn't burn that bridge before we get to it,'" Elfie said. "Right, Mommy?"

"Right." Elizabeth stood up and extended a white, slim hand to Gail. "Thank you for helping out with Elfie, Miss Durand. I probably won't see you again. We'll be flying home this afternoon."

"So soon?" Gail took the hand, then released it quickly. "Well, good luck."

Elfie ran to her and threw her arms around her waist. "I'll miss you, Miss Gail!" she cried.

Gail felt an unexpected lump in her throat. "I'll miss you, too, dear," she said.

"I'll write to you. I can write pretty good now. I can read, too. Will you write to me?"

"Of course, if you'll give me your address."

"Anyway, if you're going to work for Vince— Grandfather," she corrected with a quick glance at her mother, "we'll probably see each other again. Maybe we'll all be at the castle this summer!"

Not bloody likely! Gail thought morosely. She kissed the child and walked into the hall. Vince was just coming in from the beach, followed by Harry, carrying his chair.

"Gail!" Vince exclaimed happily. "I didn't expect you back so soon. Did you enjoy the trip?"

"It was great," she said wearily.

His eyes examined her face. "Well, I can see you won't want to do any work today, but maybe by tomorrow everything will have settled down to normal. Can you come over first thing in the morning?"

"Yes, I'll do that," she agreed.

"Why don't you pack all your things and just move over here? I'll send Harry—"

"If you don't mind, Vince, I think I'd rather stay in the apartment for the rest of the week, as I'd planned. After that, we'll see."

"You'd better plan on staying here, my dear. Rents are quite exorbitant on the island, and there's the problem of transportation if you go any farther away."

"I know, Vince. We'll talk about it later." All Gail wanted to do at the moment was to go back to the Sand Dollar and collapse.

"All right then, Gail. I'll see you in the morning. Harry, drive Miss Durand back to her apartment."

Harry nodded, put down the chair, picked up Gail's bag, and went out. She followed him.

When Gail entered the lobby of the Sand Dollar a short time later, Judy was just coming out of her office.

"Well, hi, Gail! I didn't expect you back so soon." Gail thought that if one more person said that to her, she was going to throw up. "How did it go?"

"Terrific!" Gail muttered through clenched teeth.

"Hmmm." Judy studied her with narrowed

eyes. "Then why do you look like you were about to fall on your face? I was just going to lunch. Want to join me and tell old Aunt Judy all about it?"

"No, thanks. I'm not hungry. I just want a shower and then a good long nap."

"I must say you look as though you could use both of them. Well, I'll be around if you want to talk later. Free advice and consolation and never an 'I told you so!'"

Gail gave her a feeble smile and went over to the elevators. The shower revived her to a certain extent, so she made some instant coffee and decided she'd better call her editor, Jim, and tell him of her decision. If she was going to quit, it was only fair to let him know right away.

His voice sounded so good to her that she was almost tempted to forget the whole thing and tell him she was coming home.

"Gail! Nice to hear from you. How's the weather down there?"

"Beautiful, Jim. The sun is shining and it's about 78 outside at the moment. What's it like up there?"

"Need you ask? We got two inches more snow last night. Thawing a bit today, though. How are you feeling? Getting your strength back so you can come home and slave for me some more, I hope?"

"Jim, that's why I called. I wanted to tell you that I don't think I'm coming back."

"What do you mean—not coming back? Never? You getting married or something?"

"No, of course not. And, of course, I'll come home eventually—all my things are in Wallen. But I've got a chance for a new job, and I think

I'll give it a try. It's just temporary, but you know I was thinking of trying for a job in New York City or someplace in the fall."

"Yes, I know you wanted a change, and I don't blame you. You're wasted on our little rag. But what is this temporary job you're talking about?"

She explained about Vince Shane and his memoirs. "He may tire of it in a few weeks," she concluded. "But I want to give it a try."

"Good heavens, Gail," he told her, "you know the country is cluttered with senior citizens all wanting to write the story of their life. Every established writer gets besieged with requests wanting him to read and edit their pitiful little scribblings. Don't get suckered in on something like that! There's no money in it. None of them ever get published except by the vanities."

"I know that, Jim. But this is a bit different. I mean, Vince has really been around and he's known all sorts of famous people. There just might be a book in it. Anyway, I'll know better after I've gone through his papers. I just want to give it a try. Okay? You know Irene Fulton is dying to take over my job. Give her a chance."

Jim sighed. "All right, Gail. But I'm going to miss you like hell. Let me know how it goes, okay?"

"Of course, Jim. And thanks—thanks a million for everything. I'll be in touch."

There were tears in her eyes when she hung up. Her first bridge burned. She couldn't call her aunt because she was still off cruising. She'd get in touch with her the following week. Get her to send some more of her clothes.

If Gail was really going to stay here for any length of time, she'd have to make a quick trip north and get a lot more of her things. But then she didn't know how long Vince was going to stay at Samburan.

He'd once said something about the summers being unbearable there, and this was the latest he'd ever stayed. But where was he going next? And would he want to take her with him?

Oh, dear, it was all so complicated! And why couldn't she forget the look of contempt in Leo's eyes when he said, "I thought you were different from the others."?

Who was Leo to sneer at her—a man who would actually make overtures to a woman just to get her away from his uncle and his money?

Gail dropped onto the bed and soon fell into a sleep of utter exhaustion. Several hours later she was awakened by the ringing of the telephone on the stand by the bed. Still half asleep, she picked up the receiver, her heart pounding. Was it Leo? And why did the thought of speaking to him frighten her?

"Gail? Lyle Johnson here."

"Oh—hello, Lyle." She glanced around the room blearily. What time was it? The sun was shining through the windows facing the sea; it seemed about to set.

"I'd really like to see you again before you go," Lyle was saying. "How about dinner and a movie tonight?"

"Oh, Lyle, I'm sorry. I got back from a cruise down among the islands a few hours ago and I have a terrible headache. Must have got too much sun or something. But, actually, I'm not leaving at the end of the week after all. I'm going to work with Vince Shane on his memoirs, so I'll be around for a while. How about a rain check on the movie?"

"Hey, that's terrific! I mean, that you're not going back home yet. Most of us just come down here for a vacation or something and get hooked. I'll call you later then."

"Yes, do that, Lyle."

She dropped the receiver down in place and lay on her back, one arm over her eyes. Hooked? Yes, she was hooked all right. But not by a place—by a man with blue-green eyes and no conscience— a man for whom she should feel nothing but contempt. A man who now felt only contempt for her. Oh, why did she ache with longing at the very thought of him?

CHAPTER NINE

The following morning Gail walked down the beach to the path that led to Samburan. By now some of her natural optimism had reasserted itself, and she felt ready to cope with whatever the day might bring. The only thing she really dreaded was having to face Leo's scornful gaze.

She needn't have worried; he wasn't around when she was admitted at the front door by a smiling Mary.

"Mr. Shane is expecting you," the housekeeper said. "I'll show you where he is."

She led the way through the long hall to the back veranda where Vince was sitting at the big table, with stacks of notebooks, bundles of letters, and a pile of newspaper clippings spread out before him.

"Good morning, Gail," he said cheerfully. "As

you can see, I've been getting this mess sorted. But that seems to be as far as I can go. I just sit here staring at it hopelessly. How does one go about making a coherent book out of this mess? That's why I need a professional."

She sat down in a chair beside his. "I'm not really a professional," she protested. "I've written plenty of news stories, but never a book. However, we'll have a go at it. Are they in any sort of chronological order?"

"Yes, I've tried to sort the stuff according to dates. There isn't anything recent, of course. I gave up keeping a journal long ago, and I've lost nearly all my old contacts. Mostly this material covers the period from the time I went to Europe in my late twenties, until I was in my fifties. There is some stuff that's got an earlier date. And there are big gaps. I think you'll just have to go over it and see for yourself."

"I suppose that would be best." Gail picked up a notebook dated 1942. "Were you in the war, Vince?"

"Yes, briefly, but nothing much happened to me then. I was in the Air Force and flew a few bombing missions, but not as a pilot. My vision wasn't good enough. Then I was wounded and spent most of the war in a hospital. My life really began when I went back to Europe after the war."

He waited in rather fidgety silence for a while, watching her read. Then he said: "If you don't need me, I could go to the beach for my usual morning session. You might do better if I just left you alone for a while."

"All right, Vince. Why don't you do that?"

He pushed back his chair, looking rather uncertain. "If you need a typewriter, I've fixed up sort of a little office for you in the room you'll have next week when you move in here. I'm not supposed to go upstairs, you know. But when you want to work alone, you can go up there. I don't know how much you'll want me with you."

"I'll have to ask you a lot of questions—fill in gaps here and there, clarify things, I should think."

"Yes. Well, anyway, I had Leo get you an electric typewriter. I hope that's all right."

"That's fine, Vince." So the business of her room was settled. Well, why not?

"I wanted to get a word processor, but Leo said no use to put all that money into something until we find out how it's going to go. Swedes are as bad as Scots when it comes to spending a buck, you know."

"Really, Vince, I don't need a word processor, for heaven's sake! I wouldn't even know how to use one. Our office isn't all that modern."

"That's good. Now Leo, he just uses the same old manual machine he's had for years, but as I said—"

"What does he use it for?"

"Didn't he tell you? No, he probably didn't. He's a strange, secretive son-of-a-gun. Hates to talk about himself. He inherited his father's talent for writing—has done several long historical novels about the early Vikings. He's well known in Sweden, but not over here—yet. But a big New York publisher wants to bring out his books in English, and Leo said okay if he could do the translations himself. That's what he's working on now."

"That's very interesting, Vince. The way people here talked, I thought he was just a glorified farmer."

"The estate? No, he's just running that on a temporary basis. You see, Anna Lisa—that's his mother—married a man who also had been married before and had a son, considerably older than Leo. Now he's the real heir to that estate. But when Leo was through school—he was educated over here at Princeton, by the way—his stepbrother, Erik, asked him to run the place for a few years. Erik was interested in politics—is a member of the Swedish parliament, and has to be in Stockholm when they're in session.

"Leo agreed, because it gave him plenty of time for his writing. But now Erik is planning to quit politics next year and devote his full time to the estate."

"Does Leo mind?" Gail asked.

"No, he'll be glad to be free of it. He wants to devote his full time to his writing now. I think he plans to live here at Samburan most of the year."

"What about his mother—Anna Lisa?"

"She's going to get an apartment in town. She could stay on at the estate if she wanted to— there's plenty of room—but she doesn't want to. Leo thinks she might even marry again. She's still a beautiful woman. There's a man in the town near the estate she's been seeing a lot."

"Why didn't her second husband adopt Leo? He was quite young when she married again, wasn't he?"

"Yes. But my brother, John, made her promise when he was dying that Leo would always keep the name Shane. I guess John figured I'd never have any sons." Vince sighed. "So Anna Lisa wouldn't let her second husband adopt Leo, although he was a good father to him."

Gail was really astonished at the idea of Leo as a writer. Why hadn't he told her? They had more in common than she had thought.

"Since Leo is a writer," she said, "why don't you get *him* to do your book?"

Vince gave a short laugh. "Oh, I mentioned it once, but he said he wasn't interested in doing that sort of gossipy trivia. He doesn't seem to think it has a chance of publication."

"Well," Gail said angrily, "he doesn't know everything. Maybe we can show him! It might even be a best seller!"

Vince brightened. "Do you really think so, dear girl?" He rose from the chair. "Well, you get on with it then, and I'll toddle down to the beach. If you want to go up to the room I had fixed for you, just ask Mary. She'll show you which one."

Gail watched him go with exasperated affection. If that was the limit of his attention span, she could see she'd have her work cut out for her. She continued to skim the material.

A lot of it was totally useless: inane trivia, inconsequential letters from friends, uneventful stories of parties and cruises, and so forth. But here and there she found some little gems of anecdotes, such as the hilarious account of a gondola ride with Elsa Maxwell in Venice and the unexpected encounter with Noel Coward in Bermuda. Vince had known just about everybody, it seemed.

But even some of the better stories needed filling out, and others were too malicious to publish without risking a lawsuit. The account of Vince's first marriage was touching. All in all, Gail thought that if she could get him to elaborate on the best stories, she might end up with something worth publishing.

Gail was so absorbed in her reading that she didn't hear Leo's approach up the path from the dock. Suddenly, she just looked up and found him gazing down at her with a sardonic smile.

"Has Uncle deserted you already?" he asked.

"There really isn't much he can do until I've gone through it myself," she replied defensively.

He sat down and lit a cigarette. Apparently, he'd been working on the boat, because he was wearing only shorts and had a smudge of grease on his chin.

"Well, I don't envy you the job," he said.

"I understand you've already turned it down," Gail told him.

He looked annoyed. "It's not my sort of thing," he muttered.

"Why didn't you tell me you were a writer? I find that very interesting."

"There is probably a great deal we've never told each other," he said.

"I'm sure there is," Gail replied coldly.

Mary came out with a tray containing a pot of coffee and cups. "Thought you might need a coffee break about now," she said cheerfully.

"Mary, you are a gem," Leo told her.

She laughed. "Well, I know you Swedes. Got to have your coffee."

"I practically live on it at home myself," Gail said.

Mary gave her a critical glance. "Yes, you look it, Miss Gail. Need to get more meat on your bones, honey, and that's a fact."

"What there is of it is nicely distributed, though," Leo remarked.

Mary grinned, poured out their coffee, and went back into the house.

"Vince says that you write historical novels about Vikings," Gail said conversationally.

He frowned and stirred sugar into his coffee. "Why do people always think that if it's Swedish and historical, it's got to be about Vikings? But then, of course, Vince hasn't read my books, since they're in Swedish. Actually, my first novel, the one I'm translating now, is about the island of Gotland in the fourteenth century."

"Gotland? I'm afraid I don't—"

Vince appeared in the doorway. "Good heavens, Leo, are you boring the poor girl with Swedish history? How are you getting along, my dear?"

"Quite well, I think, but you're going to have to fill in a lot of gaps for me."

"Of course, of course, but it's almost lunchtime now, and then I'll have to have my nap. I'm going to have a shower now and a massage. You might as well quit for the day—or work a while longer on your own, if you like."

Obviously Leo had been right, Gail thought. Vince didn't have the necessary discipline to settle down to any kind of real work.

"I'll go home," she told him, "and read the journals more thoroughly there."

She knew that they were the only real source of material; the letters were frivolous jottings from friends, the news clippings merely brief accounts of parties Vince had attended. He may have known a lot of famous people, but they hadn't corresponded with him.

"Just as you like, but you must have lunch before you go. Harry can run you home when I go to nap. You really ought to move in now—save a lot of trouble."

"Next Monday," she said, "when my time in the apartment is up. I believe the owner is coming home then. But it isn't necessary for anyone to drive me. I can very well walk."

"Dear girl, must you always be so energetic? The sun is too hot in the afternoon. And you'll have all those heavy journals to carry."

"I will drive you back, Gail," Leo said.

She wondered why he would bother when he so obviously disapproved of her. But perhaps he had decided to continue his wooing her away from Vince—in spite of everything.

Lunch was served on the porch, and Vince kept up his usual inconsequential chatter.

"Do you know," he said shortly before the end of the meal, "it just occurred to me that my birthday is coming up in about two weeks. My seventieth. Don't you think that rates some special sort of celebration? Good grief, I'm really getting old!"

"I really don't think you're up to any celebrating, Uncle," Leo told him.

"Nonsense! I'm not suggesting any wild orgies —just a quiet little gathering of my old friends around here—if there are any left. I used to know quite a few."

"There are still some of them around, I suppose," Leo said.

"Well, then, would it be asking too much for you to contact them? We could have it at the yacht club—of course, there isn't enough room here. I'd like to see them all once again before we leave here for the summer. After all, it may be my last chance." Vince managed to inject a rather pitiful quiver into his voice.

Leo gave him a cynical glance. "Never mind the pathetic act. If Dr. Blair says it's okay, we'll do it. But you know the rules."

"I certainly ought to by now," Vince said petulantly, but he looked considerably cheered. "It will be something to look forward to, at any rate. I'll start making out a list today, and you can find out who's available."

He went off quite happily with Harry. Leo smiled at Gail and shook his head.

"Poor chap," he said. "He just can't live without some sort of entertainment."

"Well, it must be dull for him here. You don't think a party would excite him too much?"

"I'll have to see what his doctor says. The local doctor here has all the information on Uncle's case, and he's been looking after him since we got here. He thinks he's doing quite well."

She rose and gathered up the pile of journals. "I might as well go home and get at these again."

Leo also rose and took them from her. "You really think you can get a book out of this stuff?"

"Yes, I do. It's quite amusing, a lot of it. If Vince will only cooperate."

"That's the problem, of course. I warned you about that."

When they were walking down the path toward the garage, she glanced back at the house as though aware they were being watched. She saw Harry on the screened balcony gazing down at them. An involuntary little shiver went through her.

Gail couldn't help but wonder about the man. Something about him gave her the creeps. How could he stand being on duty twenty-four hours a day, seven days a week? He seemed to have no life of his own—although she supposed Leo did take over his duties occasionally, so he could have some time off.

She spoke her thoughts aloud as she got into the car. "How can Harry stand having no private life and such long hours on duty? He seems a rather peculiar character. Do you know he never talks to me at all? Even that time he drove me home after our cruise, he never said a word the whole trip."

Leo shrugged. "Harry hates women. He had a rough childhood—his mother beat him and the authorities took him away from her and put him in a foster home. Yes, he's an oddball, but just what we needed here. Not many men would take the job. He has two days off a week and the pay is good."

"Where did you find him?"

"Dr. Blair got him for us. Actually, he's just on leave from his regular job—likes to change to private duty once in a while."

"Where is he from?"

"Miami." Leo hesitated and then added, "Actually, he isn't a nurse at all. He's an orderly in a mental institution."

Gail stared at him in horror. "But—but Vince isn't crazy!"

"No, of course not. But he does need constant supervision."

They were driving past some exotic trees, but Gail looked at them unseeingly. "Why, Leo?"

Again the hesitation. "Let's just say that the sort of life Vince was leading meant that he would not live much longer if he continued it.

Since he lacks the will power to give it up, we have to see that the old habits are not resumed."

"Why should *you* make that decision for him? Maybe he'd rather lead the life he enjoys and die with his boots on, so to speak, than drag out years of boredom and loneliness."

Leo sighed. "Unfortunately, it isn't that simple, Gail. But I'm not going to argue with you. Think what you will."

She was silent while he got out and opened the gates. When they drove on, she said: "How soon are you going back to Sweden?"

"In about four or five weeks."

"Will you take Vince with you?"

"Of course. He can hardly stay here alone. Or are you planning on taking over his care?"

She winced at the cold irony in his voice. "I'm only trying to help him with his memoirs. They seem to mean a lot to him."

"Really? He hasn't given me that impression. I'd say they're more of an idle whim."

Gail was glad when they reached the Sand Dollar and she could make her escape.

"I'll pick you up in the morning at nine," Leo said when he opened the car door for her.

"Don't bother. I'll walk."

"Not with all those journals. Don't be so stubborn."

She stood watching him drive away, then turned and hurried angrily into the building. She was glad that Judy wasn't around to waylay her.

Which of the men was telling the truth? Leo's version was that Vince would rush off and kill himself with wild living unless watched every minute. Vince's was that he was being held a virtual prisoner so that he wouldn't marry again and let a new wife take over his fortune.

Gail remembered Elfie's description of an over-heard conversation. Elizabeth had said that Leo should win her attention away from Vince even if he had to act as if he loved her. Or something to that effect. Oh, it was easy enough to know which of the Shane men was telling the truth! Leo was determined to get hold of the Shane fortune. Poor Vince! She had been right in thinking that Harry looked more like a guard than a nurse. A muscle man! And from an insane asylum at that! A man used to handling violent patients. A man who hated women! No wonder Harry gave her the creeps. The thought of living in the same house with him did not appeal to her, and yet someone had to rescue Vince from those awful people.

There was no one but her to do it.

CHAPTER TEN

During the days that followed, Gail was able to work out a fairly efficient routine to accomplish what she was trying to do. Since Vince seemed to be capable of work only when thoroughly rested, she would make notes ahead of time on the questions she wanted to ask him. Then she would query him, with a tape recorder going. He seemed to enjoy talking more than writing, and could recall by association many amusing embellishments to his written accounts.

When he tired and went off to bed or the beach, Gail would play back the conversation, typing up what she wanted to use. By the end of the week, she felt that it was going to work out if they could just keep it up long enough. Of course, it wouldn't be possible to finish even a first draft in the short time they had.

When she mentioned that to Vince, he said: "But of course not, dear girl. I never thought that we could. Later, when we go back to Europe, you must come, too, and we will finish it there."

"In Sweden? Somehow I don't think Leo would be overjoyed to have me tagging along there. And after all, it is his mother's home. She wouldn't—"

"Forget Sweden!" Vince said impatiently. "Can't stand that moldy old estate. Deadly. We'll go somewhere else, just the two of us. I'll be well enough by then. Maybe Capri. I adore Capri, although it's not at its best in the summer. We'll see."

He spoke with airy confidence, but Gail knew it wasn't going to be that easy. Leo wasn't going to let his prisoner just walk out on him like that. Not a chance. But if he did—if he did—would she go off with Vince as he suggested? She would have to think about that.

Finally, it was Saturday and Gail had the day off to clean the apartment and pack her things. It had been decided that she would move to Samburan on Sunday, not Monday. Her aunt had arrived home the night before and had called Gail to find out how she was enjoying her vacation in Florida.

When Gail had given her a carefully edited version of what had been happening and told her that she was going to stay in Florida for a while longer, her aunt was silent for a moment, then said: "I knew I'd lose you someday, but I didn't think it would happen so soon—and so suddenly."

"Oh, well, now, darling," Gail said quickly, "this whole thing could fall apart before long, and I'll be back on your doorstep. In any event, I'll make a quick trip up in a few weeks—I've got to get some more clothes—and we'll talk it over then."

She hadn't mentioned the possibility of her going to Europe with Vince, and she had lightly glossed over the attractive nephew he was living with.

"The whole thing does sound awfully chancy somehow," her aunt said doubtfully.

"Don't worry about it. I'll see you soon." She'd hung up before her aunt could ask any questions.

Judy came up just as Gail was finishing scrubbing the kitchen floor.

"You didn't have to do that," Judy protested. "We have a maid that cleans up when a tenant leaves. Of course, the owner of the apartment pays for it. Lots of owners rent them out part-time and can't be here to clean up when a tenant leaves, so we have this arrangement."

"Oh, that's all right," Gail said, wiping perspiration from her face. "I felt like doing something physical."

Judy sat down and lit a cigarette. "Got any coffee? You know, I'm not at all happy about your moving to Samburan."

Gail turned the heat on under a pot she kept ready on the stove. "Why not? Do you think they have some sinister plot to murder me and bury my body in the jungle?"

Judy shrugged. "I wouldn't put it past them. Especially that weirdo, Harry."

Gail brought two mugs over to the kitchen table. "Did you know that he's an orderly in a mental institution in Miami?"

"Really? But why did Leo hire him?"

"Well, he's good with Vince, and Harry likes a

change in his routine once in a while. They wouldn't have him there if he wasn't all right. Just because he works in a nut house doesn't make him a nut."

"I'm not so sure. I wouldn't want to live in the same house with him. And that goes for Leo and Vince, too."

"Oh, come now, Judy. They're just ordinary men." Gail opened the refrigerator and took out the cream.

"You have a strange idea of ordinary men. And the place is so isolated—all that jungle around. And the locked gate—you couldn't get away if anything happened."

"Judy, honestly! You're making it sound like a gothic novel. All I'd have to do would be to walk out along the beach. Anyway, the Forbeses are there."

"Not all the time. Sometimes they visit their daughter in Miami."

Gail turned off the heat and took off the coffee. "You're being silly, Judy."

"Maybe so, but I'll still worry about you. You will come to see me often, won't you, and let me know how things are going?"

"Of course, I will."

"And if that job deteriorates, I'll bet you could get a job on the newspaper in Naples—if you still want to stay in Florida, that is."

"I'll keep it in mind. At this point I'm not making any long-range plans."

"You doing anything tonight?"

"I told Lyle I'd go to dinner and a movie with him. I've kept putting him off, but I do like him, so I didn't want to discourage him completely."

"Well, good. If you feel like dropping in at the club later, we'll probably be there. It's our Saturday night special. The food's better and cheaper than you can get in a restaurant, and the dancing's good."

"Yes, I liked it. Vince is talking about having a party to celebrate his seventieth birthday in a couple of weeks—at the club."

"Really? I wonder who he'll invite."

"I've no idea. He wants Leo to round up some of the people he used to associate with here."

"Oh, they were mostly very rich or professional people up in Naples. But a lot of his old friends are dead or gone away now."

"I suppose so, but he seems determined to have some sort of affair."

Gail enjoyed the evening with Lyle more than she had expected to. He was really a very personable young man. They didn't go to the yacht club. They had dinner and went to a movie in Naples and then stopped in at a little nightclub in a hotel somewhere along the mainland coast between Naples and the island.

He kissed her goodnight in the lobby of the Sand Dollar and gave her a rueful smile. "I don't really register with you at all, do I, Gail?" he said. "Sometimes tonight I've had the feeling you didn't even know I was there."

She flushed. "Lyle, I'm sorry. I've got a lot of things on my mind just now. You know I like you."

"Yes, we're friends. But I was hoping for more."

"I'm sorry."

"Well, it's not your fault. I knew from the be-

ginning I wouldn't have a chance with Golden
Boy around. Maybe when he goes back to Sweden—oh, well. Can I see you again?"

"If you want to. I'll be at Samburan after tonight."

"I know—damn it! Well, goodnight, Gail." He
gave her another light kiss and went away.

She watched him go a bit regretfully. He was
probably right. If Leo hadn't been there, she
would have gone out happily with Lyle, maybe
even have fallen in love with him eventually. But
right now Gail felt Lyle could be nothing more to
her than a good friend.

Harry picked up Gail and her luggage in the
morning and took her to Samburan. Now that
she knew more of his background, she felt even
more uncomfortable with him. But as usual he
virtually ignored her and spoke only when forced
to.

Mary showed Gail to a pleasant, old-fashioned
room at the back of the house, facing the bay.
There were fresh flowers on the dresser, and in
one corner a desk had been set up with the new
electric typewriter. Gail was particularly pleased
with the French windows that opened onto the
screened balcony, which was furnished with
wicker chairs, a table, and a couch. She could
even sleep out there on warm nights if she liked.

Gail saw very little of Leo during the week
that followed. They all had their meals together,
of course, but the rest of the time he was working
in his room or off somewhere in the boat. He
seemed to put in rather long hours on his trans-
lation.

She would have loved to read some of Leo's

manuscript, but he seemed to be avoiding her, and there wasn't much opportunity to ask him. At the table Vince monopolized the conversations. Apparently, Leo had decided to treat her with carefully courteous indifference, with no more attempts to lure her away from Vince.

Vince seemed to be more interested in his upcoming birthday party than in the memoirs, although Gail was able to get him involved for an hour or so every morning after breakfast. He was very pleased that Leo had managed to contact quite a few of the people he had socialized with in the past. And the guest list had now grown to around fifty.

"Of course," Vince told Gail, "a lot of the people we're inviting aren't close friends. Some of them are just those we have business dealings with, such as our lawyer, Jay, and his wife, and Dr. Blair, and so on and so forth."

Jay and his wife, Gail noted. So one of Elizabeth's old admirers had married—apparently loving her was not a permanent or terminal disease. But had Leo recovered from it?

"And, of course, there should be some younger people there," Vince went on, "not just my old friends, because you and Leo will be there, and I think Elizabeth has promised to fly over for it. Leo was talking to her on the phone last night."

"Will she bring Elfie?" Gail asked.

"I hope not! I wouldn't think so, just for a weekend. There's adequate help at their home to look after her."

"I'm very fond of Elfie," Gail protested. "She's an unusual child."

"Spoiled rotten," Vince said. "But never mind her. I was going to ask if there was anyone you'd

like to invite while we're at it. I love a big crowd.
Isn't there someone at the Sand Dollar you were
rather chummy with?"

"Yes, the manager's niece, Judy Wood," Gail
said eagerly. She knew Judy would be thrilled to
get an invitation. "She was awfully nice to me
while I was there."

"Well, send her an invitation. There are plenty
left. Tell her to bring her boyfriend or whatever. I
presume she has one."

"Yes, she's engaged to a lawyer in Naples."

"Anyone else you'd like to ask?"

She thought of Lyle. He'd be glad to come, but
did she really want him? Of course, Leo would
have Elizabeth...

"I'll think about it," she replied. "Of course, I
don't really know anybody here yet."

Her first week at Samburan passed swiftly,
and Gail began to feel as though she had lived
there for a long time. She loved the house and its
surroundings. And in her free time, of which she
had quite a bit, she explored the beaches and the
woods on the private end of the island. Gail swam
every day, grew quite brown, and she soon felt
fully recovered from her pneumonia.

One morning early in her second week at Samburan, Gail paused in the middle of the tape she
was transcribing, hearing the unexpected sound
of music. At first she thought it was the stereo
that Leo often played, but then she realized it
was the piano in the living room.

She went soundlessly in her bare feet down the
stairs to the arched doorway. Leo was seated at
the piano, playing one of the haunting Chopin
etudes. Gail slipped into the room and sank onto

the couch without his being aware of her presence.

Leaning back and closing her eyes, she listened as he finished the etude and began something by Schumann. Then he played a show tune, followed by some Bach.

After that came some music Gail didn't recognize, something from Sweden, perhaps, reflecting the mystery and loneliness of the great spruce forests and the rocky hills where the trolls lived. Perhaps she made some sound, because the music stopped abruptly, and Leo turned to look at her with a stern, almost accusing, expression.

"Please don't stop," Gail murmured. "You play so well."

But his mood was broken and he rose abruptly. "It's only a form of relaxation," he said. "I have no real skill."

And then he was gone. She went back to the typewriter, the music echoing through her mind.

CHAPTER ELEVEN

One morning when Gail had broken off work to join Vince on the beach for a while, he said to her abruptly: "Do you have a passport?"

"Yes," she told him. "When I graduated from college, my aunt gave me a trip to Europe. I went with a group of my friends. We rented a car and had a marvelous time. I've always wanted to go back."

"You shall, my dear. I'll take you. I've been thinking about it a lot. Once this party is out of the way, we'll have to make serious plans. I heard Leo talking on the phone to Elizabeth last night —there's an extension by my bed and sometimes I eavesdrop quite shamelessly. You never know when you might pick up something useful. When one is being kept a prisoner—"

"Vince, I can't believe you are really a prisoner!"

"What would you call it then?" he demanded. "When I got out of the hospital, Leo insisted that I come here instead of going back to Cannes. A friend of mine has a villa there and I could have stayed with her and hired a nurse to look after me. But, no, Leo said I must come here for a while, and I was too weak at the time to assert myself. Then he hired that thug, Harry, to watch me every minute."

"But couldn't you leave if you wanted to now that you are stronger? How can he force you to stay here?"

"Well, I haven't been strong enough to just walk out and take a plane on my own. But now that I have you, it will be different. You can help me."

For some reason his words gave her a faint twinge of alarm. "How, Vince?"

"I'm not sure yet. Anyway, what I was starting to tell you was that I heard Leo talking to Elizabeth. She is definitely coming for the party, by the way. And she asked him how soon he was going back to Sweden, and he said about two weeks after the party. Then she asked what he intended to do about you. Would you go along, or what? And he said, 'No, Liz.' These were his exact words. 'I must find some way to separate them before then. It would be too dangerous.' And she said, 'Well, good luck, darling. I'll see you soon.' And she hung up. So you see, Gail, we'll have to make some plans of our own."

Vince's pale-blue eyes were glittering with excitement and he reached out to put his bony hand on her arm.

"We'll go somewhere for the summer, just the two of us, some place that is cool and beautiful — and we will finish the memoirs. And I'll get well again. I'll work it out. They can't stop us!"

Gail was beginning to be alarmed by the feverish flush on his cheeks and the gleam in his eyes. It couldn't be good for his heart to get so worked up.

"All right, Vince," she said soothingly, "but calm down now. You know it's bad for you to get so excited."

He leaned back in his chair with a sigh. "I know. I know. And we mustn't let them suspect we're planning anything. Leo is clever. He'd find a way to stop us. I'm letting him think I'm resigned to going to Sweden with him. But you go up right now and write to your aunt and tell her to send you the passport. We need to be ready when the time comes."

"All right, Vince. But I had thought to take a few days off and fly home. I need to get some more clothes, and I could pick up the passport then."

"No, Gail!" The frantic look came back into his eyes. "You can't do that! That's all Leo would need. He'd whisk me away before you got back. I'll give you some money and you can buy what you need. But get that passport as soon as you can."

"All right, Vince. I'll go and write now."

She went back to her room, Leo's words seething through her mind. So Leo was trying to figure out some way of getting rid of her, was he! But what could he do?

Leo and Elizabeth — plotting together — oh, it was all so humiliating! But they would find that she wasn't so easy to get rid of—and she would save Vince from their greedy schemes. But she must be very careful and not let Leo know that she suspected anything.

She sat down at her desk and began the letter to her aunt.

The next few days passed uneventfully. Gail had lunch at the Sand Dollar with Judy, who was elated at being invited to the birthday celebration. Gail also paid a visit to her aunt's friend, Mrs. Collins, to thank her for the use of her condo. She worked very hard on the memoirs, although it was hard to get Vince to concentrate on them now. All his attention was turned onto his approaching party.

The party was to be on a Friday night, and Elizabeth was scheduled to fly in on Thursday afternoon. The Sunday evening before, Leo stopped by Gail's room on his way to get cleaned up for dinner, after a day's fishing.

He said: "If you'd like to see something of the Everglades while you're here, I thought we could take a drive over tomorrow. Of course, to do it right one should spend several days. But at least you could get some idea of what it's like. If we start right after breakfast, we can be back by evening."

She was surprised by the invitation, and a little suspicious. Was this part of his scheme to separate her from Vince? But what could he do on a sight-seeing trip to the Everglades—short of tossing her into the swamp? And she hardly thought he was that desperate. It annoyed her that the thought of spending a day with him had the power to make her heart beat faster, to send a thrill of excitement through her veins.

"But I'm supposed to be working tomorrow," she said.

"You hardly ever take a day off. You were even hard at it today," he accused. "Anyway, tomorrow Harry is taking Vince to a clinic in Naples to have some tests run for Dr. Blair. They'll be gone all morning, and he'll be exhausted when he gets home and have to go to bed. It will be a good chance to get away."

Leo gave her a friendly smile. And while she didn't trust him for a moment, she couldn't resist —either the chance to spend a day with him, or to see the Everglades.

"All right," Gail agreed. "What time?"

"An early start—maybe seven? I'll tell Mary we'll want breakfast at six and she can pack us a lunch."

The day was bright and beautiful. Although it was a bit on the cool side when Gail got up, she knew it would be warm by afternoon. She put on shorts and a T-shirt and packed her canvas bag with the things she'd need for the day: camera, wallet, sunglasses, and so on. She even stuffed in a sweater in case it got cooler in the evening.

Vince was still in bed when they left, but the night before when she'd told him of Leo's invitation, he'd warned her: "I don't know what he's up to, but whatever he may suggest, pretend to go along with it. And don't trust him for a minute, dear girl!"

They were driving through the Everglades— with Gail admiring the grassy swamp, the birds in the cypress trees, the primitive power of all the jungle vegetation surrounding them—when

Leo asked: "How are Vince's memoirs going?"

"Better than I expected. If I could just get him to spend more time with me—"

"I warned you about that. So you really think there is a publishable book in them?"

Gail considered her answer carefully. "I can't be positive. Can one ever? You should know what an unpredictable business writing is. But I think there's a good chance, yes. You know, Leo, your uncle really has led an interesting life in his own way. Not only in France, but all over Europe and other places, too. And even today many Americans think of Europe as an exotic, fascinating place. So you've got a lively playboy, glamorous people, plenty of celebrities—and adventures all over Europe. A lot of American readers would just eat that up."

"You seem to have thought it out very carefully. Being half European myself, I haven't been so aware of it, I suppose. But, yes, I think you're right. To many Americans, Europe is an intriguing, sometimes mysterious, place. As for myself, I feel at home in both worlds. In fact, I may make Florida my permanent base one of these days."

"Vince—or was it you?—told me that your stepbrother will be taking over the Swedish estate in another year or so."

"That's right, and I will be very pleased when he does. I've only stayed on because they needed me. I'd rather devote all my time to my writing. Of course, I'll always spend my summers there, I suppose."

"And you're going back there quite soon."

He gave her a slanting glance. "Yes, I have to. In about three weeks."

"And you're taking Vince with you, of course."

"That's what I wanted to talk to you about. I suppose he has told you that he wants you to go with him."

"And you don't want me there, of course," Gail replied coldly.

"It isn't a question of that. It's—well, to be blunt about it, Gail, I'm sure Uncle isn't ready to be on his own yet. And it's rather a strain keeping an eye on him all the time. I can do it here—"

"Because you have a nice, ready-made little prison there at Samburan!"

"If you want to call it that. In Sweden it will not be so easy. I am afraid he will have to stay in a sanatorium for a while. There is a very good one in Denmark, just across the straits, and I can visit him often. But, of course, you could not be with him there."

"I see. He must go from one prison to another. Have you told him this yet?"

Leo sighed. "No, not yet. He thinks I am taking him to the estate. Which he loathes, by the way. He won't like it, but there's nothing else I can do. I've talked it over with Elizabeth."

"I'm sure you have. And so what all this is leading up to, of course, is that after the next three weeks I am out of a job. Right?"

"Not necessarily. From what you tell me of the memoirs, you might really make something out of them. It would seem a pity not to go on with the project. So what I was going to suggest was that you stay on at Samburan for the summer and try to finish the book. Who knows? It might be such a success that you won't have to worry about finding another job!"

"I doubt that," she said dryly. "But what about the help I need from Vince?"

"I don't think you're getting much as it is. Can't you flesh it out yourself from all the material? And there is always correspondence—not to mention the telephone. I'll pay for the calls."

Which is really saying something, coming from a tightfisted Swede! she thought. He really must be anxious to keep an ocean between herself and Vince. But of course he was. The Shane fortune must be safeguarded at all costs.

So Leo would do anything to keep her away from Vince, even to wooing her himself—well, she would do almost anything to thwart him! She'd even go to Europe with Vince!

"You will continue with your present salary, of course," Leo went on. "You can live at Samburan and Mary will look after you."

His calm tone infuriated her. "I'm a big girl now," Gail said. "Nobody has to look after me."

"I only meant," he said, "that Mary would run the household, leaving you free for your work. Of course, if you don't care for Florida, you could go home and finish the memoirs there. Whatever you prefer."

"And what if Vince refused to go to this—this sanatorium?" she demanded.

"He can't refuse," Leo said.

"Why can't he?"

"There are reasons I can't go into now. You'll have to take my word for it."

"I'll have to think about it," Gail said wearily.

"All right, there's plenty of time."

They drove on in silence for a while, the strange beauty of the Everglades marshland working its magic on Gail's soul. She temporarily forgot her anger at Leo and her hurt. Human emotions seemed so petty in a place that had gone on for thousands and thousands of years, and would probably go on for thousands more.

Leo stopped the car in a parking area, and they took a walk on one of the trails. Gail shot several pictures and Leo pointed out some of the many birds and other animals, including a few alligators.

Later they found a picnic table and ate the lunch Mary had packed for them. The afternoon was devoted to more sight-seeing.

Finally, they walked slowly back to the car. Leo stopped to glance at Gail for a moment, a strange look on his face. Suddenly he put his arms around her and drew her close in a fierce embrace. She didn't try to break away, but just stood there, letting him hold her, her cheek against his chest.

"Oh, Gail, Gail," he murmured. "I wish..."

When she looked up at him, wonderingly, he released her.

"Never mind," he said. "We'd better be starting back to Samburan."

CHAPTER TWELVE

In the morning Gail followed Vince to the beach. She felt that she had to tell him what Leo was planning. He hadn't asked her not to tell Vince, and it was only right that he know about it, anyway. She expected Vince to become angry and upset when she told him, but he took it very calmly, almost with indifference.

"I knew he had something like that in mind," he told Gail. "You see how it is. He can't keep a close enough watch over me on the estate, so he'll put me away in a safe place until I die—probably of boredom. But it doesn't have to happen—not if you'll help me, dear girl."

"Of course, I'll help you, Vince. But you are quite sure you're strong enough to stand a trip to Europe on your own? And do you know what you'll do when you get there?" She was beginning to have a few qualms about it.

He looked annoyed. "Of course, I'm strong enough! I flew here with Leo when I was a lot weaker than I am now, didn't I? And I would be flying back soon in any event—without Harry. He's going back to his regular job in that nut house in Miami. Perfect setting for him. You and I will manage very well. I'll make arrangements for us to go to my friend in Cannes. Later we'll find a place of our own. Don't forget to pack the memoirs."

"But, Vince, how are we going to get away from here without Leo or Harry knowing?"

"Don't worry about it. I'll let you know when the time comes. I'm working it out. For now I just want to concentrate on my party. I want it to be something they'll remember for a long time—like the old days when my father used to get people here from all over the country for one of his affairs. Did I ever tell you about the time..." He wandered off into one of his lengthy reminiscences.

On Thursday Leo went to the airport to pick up Elizabeth. Elizabeth greeted Gail cordially enough when she and Leo came into the house. Obviously, she and Leo had had a good chat on the way home, and she was quite satisfied that everything was under control, and that Vince would soon be tucked away where no predatory females could get at him.

"How is Elfie?" Gail asked her.

"Oh, very well, thank you. She sent you her love."

Elizabeth went on to her room to unpack and start a long round of telephone calls.

Vince was napping and Gail decided to take a walk up to the shopping center of the island to buy a new pair of shoes for the party. She intended to wear the same dress she had worn to the yacht club before, but this time she wanted some elegant new shoes to go with it. And while she was there, she could stop in to see Judy for a few minutes.

There weren't very many shops on the island, but the best dress shop did carry a small line of shoes as well, and Gail found a pair of pale-yellow pumps that would look lovely with the dress. Then she walked over to Judy's office.

"Gail, I've been dying to see you. Let's go get some coffee."

They went in the coffee shop and Judy ordered coffee and an eclair.

"I might as well live it up today," she said. "I'm going on a diet next Monday for sure."

Judy was always going on a diet Monday for sure, Gail thought with a smile. But by Wednesday she was always back with the goodies.

"No, I really mean it this time," Judy insisted, catching the smile. "I have to lose at least ten pounds before June. Jeff and I are getting married on the nineteenth and I don't want to look like a cow in my wedding gown."

"Judy! How wonderful!" Gail was delighted, yet couldn't help but feel a pang of envy. "I know you and Jeff will be very happy."

"Well, we've been going together for over a year now, and we're getting tired of all the commuting between here and Naples. We've considered ourselves engaged for a while—and now we've decided to set the date."

Gail said, "So I suppose you'll be leaving the Sand Dollar and living in Naples."

"Yes, I'll move into his apartment for a start.

As soon as we can afford it, we want to buy a house. I hope you'll still be around here in June —I'd love to have you for my maid-of-honor."

"I'm honored, Judy, but I—I'm not sure where I'll be by June."

Gail wished that she could tell Judy everything, but she didn't dare. The whole situation seemed so unreal anyway; she couldn't quite believe she was going to Europe with Vince in a short time. She knew Judy would be horrified at the idea.

"I don't suppose the Shanes will be staying here much longer, will they?" Judy asked.

"No, Leo has to go back to his mother's estate."

"And what about Vince? Is Leo taking him along?"

"I suppose so." She didn't want to tell her about the sanatorium either.

"Well, what about this book you're working on? Will you give up on that?"

"Not necessarily. Leo suggested that I stay on at Samburan to finish it."

"Hey, that would be great! Then you *would* be around for the summer."

"I'm not sure yet what I want to do. Are you going away for a honeymoon?" She wanted to get Judy onto another subject.

"You'd better believe it! I only intend to get married once and I want to do it right. We're not sure where yet, though. Maybe a cruise. We'll see. Well, what are you going to wear to the party tomorrow night?"

Once launched on the subject of clothes, Judy was safely away from questions about Gail's future. And they chatted happily for a little while longer.

* * *

Elizabeth and Leo went to the yacht club early on Friday to supervise the final party preparations. Vince and Gail would be driven over by Harry later. She had decided not to invite Lyle. Since it was Vince's birthday, she preferred to spend most of her time with him. She had already given him her present—a beautiful little leather volume of *The Rubaiyat* that she had found in a bookstore in Naples.

Vince seemed very touched by the gift. "Ah, yes—'the Fire of Spring,'" he said. "You remembered our first conversation."

It was to be a white-jacket affair for the men and formals for the women. Gail hoped her ankle-length dress would be adequate. Elizabeth had brought a new gown for the occasion, a form-fitting ivory organza, and looked ravishingly beautiful, as usual. Leo looked very distinguished, but somehow his eyes had seemed to hold a sad expression when he'd looked at Gail just before he and Elizabeth left the house.

Gail was still thinking of Leo's eyes much later when she was fully dressed for the party and went slowly downstairs in the new shoes. Vince and Harry were waiting. They were both in white jackets and even Harry looked almost handsome.

Vince took Gail's hands and smiled at her admiringly. "My dear," he said, "you look charming. Enough to make a tired old man wish he were forty years younger."

"Thank you, Vince," she said. "You look pretty nifty yourself."

Harry stared at Gail with his cold green eyes and said nothing.

"Here," Vince said, picking up a box from the table in the hall, "these are for you."

It was a spray of delicate white flowers. "Oh, Vince, they're lovely." She fastened them to her bodice.

Vince's eyes were sparkling with pleasure at the prospect of an evening out. "Well, let's be off," he said. "After all, this is my party and I don't want to be late."

Leo had left the Mercedes for them, and Gail and Vince got into the back seat. Vince took her hand and smiled at her.

"I'm glad you didn't invite an escort," he told her. "You're my girl for the evening." Then he told her some amusing anecdotes about a restaurant in Cannes.

Gail hardly recognized the yacht club, it was so festively arrayed with flowers and colored lanterns. There was a ten-piece orchestra on the dais, softly playing French love songs. Leo and Elizabeth were waiting for Vince, and a comfortable chair had been placed near the entrance where he could sit to receive his guests.

Leo's eyes flickered over Gail briefly and he said: "You look lovely tonight."

"Thank you." Her eyes held his for a moment, as though she were sending him a wordless appeal, but for what she didn't know.

Then the guests started coming in, and for a while she was kept busy being introduced to Vince's friends. He insisted that she stand beside him with Leo and Elizabeth as part of the receiving line.

Many of them were elderly people, contemporaries of Vince, but there were also a number of young couples, including Elizabeth's lawyer, Jay, and his attractive young wife, who looked as though she spent most of her time on a tennis court.

Gail was happy to greet Judy and Jeff, and to introduce them to Vince. Judy looked radiant in a pale-green silk gown. All the people were handsomely dressed, and Vince was in his element, greeting them, exchanging quips and reminiscences about the old days.

Leo, Gail noticed, kept in the background, smiling and being courteous to all, but with a remote, withdrawn look in his eyes.

Vince always had a crowd around him, with Harry discreetly behind his chair, watching to see that he had nothing to drink but the nonalcoholic fruit punch. Waiters, meanwhile, circulated with champagne and canapes.

Gail found herself with Judy and Jeff at one point, and Judy gave her arm a little squeeze.

"Lovely party," she murmured. "Thanks for getting us invited." She took a glass of champagne from a passing waiter and raised it. "To the future!" she said. "Whatever it may bring."

The future? Gail sipped her own champagne and found herself unable to contemplate the future. It loomed in the background, big and black and frightening. What was she getting herself into?

Later there was a lavish buffet dinner, which they ate at little tables out on the terrace. Then everyone who wanted to dance crowded into the ballroom, and those who just wanted to talk found themselves seats. Vince still had his group of elderly friends around him, and Gail felt that she had no place among them.

Elizabeth and Leo started off dancing together, but were cut in on almost immediately. Gail had no lack of partners herself, although her eyes kept straying over the other heads seeking out the one gleaming blond one that stood out for her like a beacon.

Then, suddenly, the orchestra was playing "I'll See You Again," and she was in Leo's arms, moving through the crowd as though they were alone in a deserted ballroom.

"They're playing this for us," he said lightly, his arms drawing her close.

She felt his magnetism, his strength, with her head pressed against his heart. They finished the dance in silence. Then Leo stood looking down at her for a moment, his eyes boring through her. Finally, he made his little bow, thanked her, and walked away. She watched him go through a blur of tears.

Now the crowded ballroom seemed intolerable to Gail, and she slipped out to the terrace where a cool breeze was blowing. There were a few people out there, some in little groups at the tables, some in more secluded areas, so she left the terrace and walked over to the edge of the beach, where she found a stone bench in the shelter of a cluster of Australian pines.

Gail sat there, hidden by the shadows, gazing at the moon shining on the water, dissolved in futile longing. If only Leo would follow her—take her in his arms—but he didn't come.

After a while she heard voices and a couple came walking up from the beach, the young woman hanging on the man's arm, laughing up at him. She was carrying her shoes and her feet were bare. Gail didn't remember who they were, but they were part of Elizabeth's set. They didn't see her, and they started to kiss.

But the young woman pulled away quickly and said: "We'd better go in before my husband starts looking for me. By the way, what do you think about our Liz? Is she shedding her mad Hungarian and coming back to Leo, do you suppose? They certainly looked chummy tonight."

"Who knows?" the man replied. "But what do you think about old Vince and his latest acquisition—secretary or whatever. Thought he was too sick for that sort of thing, but I guess there's life in the old boy yet."

"Maybe she's Leo's girl," the young woman said.

"If she is, Leo's a lucky devil. Imagine having two beautiful creatures like that around the house!"

The girl gave him a playful slap. "Stan, you're impossible. I'll bet you'd have a harem if you could afford it. Anyway, I don't think she's Leo's because everyone says he's still carrying a torch for Liz. He's never married after all these years. And I'll bet Liz still has a thing for him—who could blame her? Oh, what a beautiful man! And here I am, stuck with you—and my husband, of course. Poor me! Some girls have all the luck."

They went on toward the terrace and Gail clasped her hands together to still their trembling. Was that what people were thinking about her—that she must belong to one of the Shane men?

Well, why not? It was true in a way. In some peculiar fashion her life had become entangled with the lives of both men, and she could not free herself. The shock receded, leaving her drained and lethargic. What difference did it make what anyone thought? In a few minutes she rose and went back to the ballroom.

Because of Vince's fragile health, the evening ended shortly after midnight with everyone singing "Happy Birthday" to him, and making a round of toasts. Gail rode home again with Vince and Harry. Vince was quiet on the way.

"Do you think it was too much for you, Vince?" she asked.

"No, dear girl, I'm all right. A bit tired, of course, but it was good to be out again." His thoughts seemed to drift to a place where she could not follow.

Back in her room, Gail undressed slowly and hung up the dress in the closet. She turned out the light and lay on her bed, but sleep seemed far away. She was too keyed up, and thoughts buzzed through her head like a swarm of angry bees. She kept hearing the laughing voice of the young woman on the beach, and seeing Elizabeth swirling around in Leo's arms. Was he still carrying a torch for her as the girl had said?

Gail felt as though she would never sleep again. Finally, she got up and slipped into her bathing suit. Maybe a swim would help calm her down, although she knew it was dangerous to swim alone, especially at night. At this point she didn't even care.

When she reached the beach with the help of a flashlight, she took a short, delicious swim, then headed back to the shore.

"Gail, what the hell are you doing?" Leo demanded.

"Just having a little swim," she said defensively.

"In the middle of the night?"

"I couldn't sleep—for that matter, what are *you* doing here?"

"Taking a walk. I couldn't sleep either. Don't you know you shouldn't swim alone at night? Or at any time, you crazy little fool!"

Suddenly his arms were around her and his mouth came down on hers in a hard, angry kiss.

"Gail," he murmured, "I thought—oh, don't you know how much I want you?"

His kisses sent shock waves of fire coursing through her veins. For one frantic moment she wanted only to remain in his arms forever. But the moment passed.

"No!" she cried, pulling herself away from his embrace. "No, Leo, it won't work! Leave me alone—just leave me alone!" And she went running away from him, back toward the house.

CHAPTER THIRTEEN

Gail woke up late feeling exhausted and depressed. She didn't want to get up, didn't want to face Leo again. But since she couldn't stay in bed forever, she got up, took a shower, and dressed. Nobody seemed to be around, so she went out to the kitchen where Mary was washing some dishes.

"Is there any coffee?" Gail asked her.

Mary looked up and smiled. "In the coffee maker, Miss Gail. You look a bit peaked this morning. Too much party last night?"

"Too much champagne, I guess," Gail admitted. "I'm not used to it. Where is everybody?"

"Mr. Vince is still in bed—tired himself out, poor soul. Mr. Leo and Miss Elizabeth have gone off somewhere. Don't you want some breakfast?"

"No, thanks. I'll just have some coffee now, I

think." Gail helped herself to a cup and wandered out to the back veranda where she sat sipping the coffee and gazing down toward the water.

In a few minutes she heard Vince's voice in the kitchen talking to Mary. Then he came out to the veranda. He was dressed in his usual beach attire—bathing trunks, short jacket, and sunglasses. She had rather expected him to be ill today after the strain of his party, but he looked quite chipper.

"Ah, there you are, Gail," he said. "When you've had your breakfast, come down to the beach with me. I want to talk to you—in private."

She felt a little pang of dismay. What did he want to tell her? "Aren't you going to eat anything?" she asked.

"I had coffee and a roll in my room. Come down when you're finished." He went back inside and through the house to the front door.

Gail finished her coffee slowly, then followed him. She met Harry on the path, coming back from establishing Vince in his chair on the beach. He gave her his usual veiled glance, then went on without speaking.

Blast the man, anyway! she thought. Why did he have to act so—so, well, weird?

At least he didn't frighten her anymore; she had come to the conclusion that he was a harmless eccentric.

She sat down on the sand beside Vince, under the shade of his beach umbrella.

"Did you enjoy my party last night?" Vince asked.

"It seemed to be a huge success," she said,

evading a direct answer. "Everybody seemed to have a good time."

"Well, it was a bit on the dull side, I thought, but then, of course, I wasn't drinking. Gail, the time has come when we have to make definite plans. I've been waiting for the right moment, and it looks as though it's nearly here. I heard Leo and Elizabeth talking this morning—I can hear a lot from my room, you know, if I leave the door ajar—and she was saying that she's going to stay over a couple of days and then go to Miami on Wednesday to visit some friends she has in Palm Beach, and then fly home from there."

Gail felt more depressed than ever. She'd been looking forward to getting rid of Elizabeth in another day.

"She asked Leo if he would drive her over, and he said he would, and that he'd take the Forbeses along, too, because they'd been wanting to visit their married daughter, who lives in Miami. I don't think Elizabeth was too thrilled about that, but she couldn't very well object. So, you see, Gail, how it's all working out. That means on Wednesday everybody will be gone except Harry. We'll never have a better chance."

She looked at him in dismay. "A chance for what?"

"Why, to get away, of course," Vince said impatiently.

"You mean—we'll run away without telling anyone?"

"Of course. Surely you don't think Leo would let me go if he knew about it?"

"But, Vince—how could he stop you? You're a grown man."

"Gail, believe me, he could stop me. Don't ask me to explain—just take my word for it. Haven't you seen how I've been kept here—a virtual prisoner with never a moment's privacy or freedom? Harry never takes his eyes off me. They're so afraid I'll slip out of their grasp."

"Vince, surely Leo just wants to take care of you! After your heart attack—"

"It was a very mild one. Not a major coronary. I'm all right now. But this is no way to live—I might as well be dead. I've got to get away, Gail. I'm not senile, I'm still a man, with the right to do as I please! Don't you agree, my dear?"

"Yes, of course. But—"

"But what? Do you mean you don't want to help me anymore? Has Leo been getting to you—"

"No, Vince! But I wouldn't want to do anything to endanger your health."

"Gail, believe me, I'm fine now. And once we get to Europe, they can't do a thing. Do you have your passport yet?"

"No, but I'm sure it will come Monday. My aunt is very prompt about replying, and I told her I wanted it right away."

"Good. I'll find a moment when nobody is around and call the airport in Fort Myers and make reservations for Wednesday. You can drive, I presume?"

"Yes, of course."

"Leo will probably take the Mercedes to Miami, so we'll have to borrow Harry's car. We'll leave a note saying he can pick it up at the airport."

"But Harry will still be here and, as you say,

he never takes his eyes off you. What are you going to do about him?"

"Don't worry about Harry. I'll take care of him when the time comes."

"But what—"

"I said, don't worry about it! It will all work out. You'll see."

Gail didn't like the feverish glitter in his eyes. The whole situation was making her more and more uneasy. To keep her resolution firm, she had to think about Leo and the way he had tried to manipulate her. He had to be punished— didn't he?

"We can be married when we get to Europe," Vince was saying. "There won't be time before."

"Married?" she said blankly.

"Oh, I know—this isn't a very romantic proposal, but that is what you want, isn't it, Gail? After all, this is more or less a business arrangement, there's no use to pretend otherwise. It will get me free of Leo and Elizabeth, and I'll make you my heir, of course. We'll both benefit."

She shook her head slowly. "I'm sorry, Vince," she said, "but I can't marry you."

He looked at her in astonishment. "But I thought that's what you've had in mind all along," he said.

"I like you. I want to help you," she told him. "I *will* help you to get away from here, Vince, if that's what you want. I'll go to Europe with you and we'll finish the book. But that will be the end of it. We're business partners, that's all. After that, I'll find a job somewhere."

He was looking at her rather oddly now. There was something—could it be relief?—in his eyes.

"Well, that's up to you, my dear," he said. "If you will help me get to Europe, I have friends there we can stay with until we decide where we want to go. The main thing is to get away from here."

"Yes, of course, I'll help you," Gail promised. "And we will finish that book."

Gail saw very little of Elizabeth and Leo during the next few days. Elizabeth was usually off somewhere with friends, and Leo was either with her or holed up in his room working. He seemed to be avoiding her, Gail thought, and she was grateful. The less they saw of each other, the better.

The passport came Monday, as expected, along with a very worried letter from her aunt, wanting to know more of what was going on—wanting Gail to come home for a visit before doing anything rash.

Gail didn't know how to reassure her—she was just as concerned about the Europe business as her aunt, actually, but she had gone too far to back out now. She wrote her aunt that she probably wouldn't stay in Europe very long—just long enough to get Vince safely established with his friends. She said she didn't really think he'd want to work on the memoirs once he left the island, although personally she still hoped to finish them.

On Tuesday evening Gail went to the beach for a last brief swim, and when she came out of the water, Leo was waiting for her.

Her heart gave a lurch of surprise—and alarm. Did he suspect something?

She picked up her towel and rubbed her hair

vigorously, trying not to meet his intent gaze.

"Will you be in Miami very long?" she asked him.

He sat down on a piece of driftwood and lit a cigarette. "Only a couple of days," he replied. "The Forbeses want to spend the weekend with their daughter and take a bus home next Monday, and I told them that would be all right. But I'll probably drive home on Friday. Do you think you could help with the cooking over the weekend?"

"Of course," she said stiffly.

It wasn't easy to stand there lying to him. But what else could she do? She couldn't say, "Sorry, but I'll be in Europe with Vince by then."

"Have you thought over what I suggested— that you spend the summer here after we've gone?" he asked.

"Yes, I've thought about it," Gail said. "But I'm not sure yet. I'll let you know in another week or so."

His eyes continued to probe into hers. Did he think she wanted to put off a decision until she knew whether or not she'd get a better offer— from Vince?

Then Leo sighed and stood up. "All right, Gail. Perhaps someday I'll be able to explain what this was all about. It's very difficult."

He walked off slowly along the beach, looking somehow so lonely.

She wanted to run after him, to throw herself into his arms crying, "I love you, Leo! I just want to be with you."

But, of course, she couldn't.

Gail went up to her room and got dressed, thinking that it was still early enough to take a walk over to the Sand Dollar. She hated the idea of leaving without saying goodbye to Judy, who had been such a good friend to her. When she went downstairs again, Vince beckoned to her from the doorway of his room.

"Harry's gone out to check something on his car," he said, "and Leo's gone off somewhere. I just wanted to tell you, when you go to your room tonight, get everything packed and ready to go. I can't pack until tomorrow, but I'm not taking much. They'll be leaving right after breakfast, but I don't think we can get away until after lunch. There's the matter of Harry—"

"You still haven't told me what you're going to do about him."

"You'll find out tomorrow. I told you not to worry about it."

"Have you called the airport?" Gail asked.

"No, I haven't had a chance. That will have to wait. There should be vacancies this time of year. The main thing is to get away from here. I think I hear Harry coming back now." Vince slipped back into his room and she went out to the beach. Leo was nowhere in sight when she headed for the Sand Dollar.

Judy was in the coffee shop finishing a late dinner when Gail got there, and she called to her to come in and have a cup of coffee.

"I'm glad you came over," Judy said. "I've been wanting to tell you how much we enjoyed Vince's party. Is Elizabeth still here?"

"Yes, but Leo is driving her to Miami tomorrow," Gail told her, sipping her coffee. "She'll fly back to L.A. from there."

"Must be nice, being able to flit hither and yon

at will," Judy sighed. "Is something wrong, Gail? You look a bit worried tonight."

Gail wondered how much she could tell Judy. She needed to talk to someone, but Vince had said no one must know of their plans. Surely she could trust Judy not to tell anyone.

She looked around the room. All the other diners had left except one elderly couple in a far corner.

"This is in the strictest confidence, Judy," she began hesitantly.

"Of course! You know I won't breathe a word!" Judy's eyes were glistening with the excitement of learning a secret.

"Well—Vince has been very unhappy with the way he's been kept practically a prisoner at Samburan. You know, with Harry breathing down his neck all the time. He says he's well enough now to go back to his old haunts—somewhere on the Riviera, I guess—but Leo won't let him. Leo is going to put him in some private sanatorium when he goes back to Sweden soon. Of course, Vince doesn't want to go to Sweden, and why should he, when he's no longer ill?"

Judy frowned and lit a cigarette. "How can Leo put him in if he doesn't want to go?" she asked. "What kind of a hold does he have over him?"

"I don't know, Judy. No one has told me. Even Vince won't explain. He just says he wants to get away from Leo, and he wants me to help him. He thinks Leo is afraid he might marry again, you see. That's why Leo's keeping him isolated."

Judy's frown deepened. "It all sounds sort of screwy to me, Gail," she said. "How does Vince expect you to help him?"

Gail drew a deep breath. "Everyone will be gone from Samburan tomorrow except Harry, Vince, and me. The Forbeses are going to Miami, too. Vince has some scheme to get Harry out of the way for a while—I don't know what—and I'm to drive Vince to the Fort Myers airport. From there we'll fly to France. He has a friend in Cannes we can stay with until we find a place to stay and finish the memoirs."

"Wow! You mean you're going with him?" Judy cried.

"Not so loud, Judy," Gail protested, looking around uneasily at the old couple. "Yes, I'm going with him."

"In what capacity?" Judy demanded.

"Only as a co-author and companion. He did ask me to marry him, but I turned him down."

"Well, I'm glad you've got that much sense, anyway!" Judy pulled deeply on the cigarette and glared at her friend.

"He doesn't have any designs on me, Judy, if that's what you're thinking. He just sees me as a way out of his difficulties. He's not strong enough to run away on his own."

"And just why are you telling me all this?" Judy demanded. "Certainly not because you want my advice—which would be to forget it and get the heck out of there while you can!"

"I don't know," Gail said miserably. "I guess I just needed someone to talk to. You really think I'm crazy to do it?"

"Worse than that—the whole thing stinks!" Judy stubbed out the cigarette in the ashtray as though it were a cockroach she was trying to kill. "There are too many things you don't understand. Why Vince lets Leo push him around—

and what Leo's real motives are! You could be getting yourself into one helluva mess, you know."

"But I want to finish the memoirs, Judy. I've really got quite involved with them and think we might do well with them."

Judy stared at her with shrewd eyes. "And I think what you're really doing is punishing Leo for something—something he did or maybe didn't do! Am I right?"

Gail flushed and clenched her hands in her lap. "I suppose that's about it," she admitted.

"And you're determined to go through with it—no matter what I say?"

"Yes, Judy, I am." She felt tears not far away.

Judy continued to stare at her for another moment, then held out her hands, and Gail put hers in them.

"Then all I can do is wish you luck, my friend —and, by heaven, you're going to need it!"

CHAPTER FOURTEEN

After a troubled and virtually sleepless night, Gail fell into an exhausted slumber toward morning. She was awakened by the sounds of departure from the yard beneath her side window. Still half asleep, she stumbled over to the window and saw the Mercedes drive away.

Well, Gail thought, she hadn't had a chance to tell any of them goodbye, but that hardly mattered now. The knowledge that she might never see Leo again filled her with anguish, but then she realized that of course she would see him again. He was sure to track them down, wherever they went, and there would be a confrontation of some sort—but she wasn't going to worry about that now.

A glance at her bedside clock told her that it was seven-forty-five. They were getting a fairly early start. How long would it take to drive to Miami? About three hours?

She took a cold shower to wake herself up and went downstairs. Everything was very neat and orderly. Even in a rush to get off, Mary would have tidied things up.

Harry was in the kitchen fixing Vince's tray.

"Good morning, Harry," Gail said, trying to sound cheerful and unconcerned.

"'Morning." Sometimes he did grant her the honor of a few monosyllables. "There's still some scrambled eggs if you want 'em." He grabbed up the tray and went out.

Would wonders never cease! Harry had actually offered her eggs. Gail went over and peered into the frying pan. Yes, there were some scrambled eggs in it. Still warm. Even some bacon draining on a paper towel at the back of the stove. She got a plate, helped herself to eggs and bacon, put some bread in the toaster, and poured herself some coffee. When all was ready, she carried it out onto the back veranda to the big table.

It was a beautiful morning. Birds were singing in a big live oak near the back porch. The earth seemed peaceful. And Gail was terrified.

In a little while Vince came out to join her.

"They got off safely, Harry tells me," he said.

"Yes, I saw them leave. What do we do now?"

He glanced nervously around. Harry was in the kitchen rinsing the breakfast dishes.

Vince leaned toward her and said softly: "Nothing yet. Everything must be as normal as possible this morning. We'll work on the book a while, then go to the beach. After lunch—"

"Yes? What then?"

"You'll see!" Vince nodded mysteriously.

The morning seemed endless. Then they had a light lunch, which she had helped Harry prepare. Harry seemed to be mellowing a bit and actually spoke to her a few times. The three of them ate together at the big table on the back veranda.

When Harry had poured their coffee, Vince said: "Oh, Harry, I left my sunglasses in my room when I was changing for lunch, and I'm getting a headache. Get them for me, will you? There's a good chap."

Harry went into the house to find the glasses. As soon as he had gone through the kitchen, Vince whipped a little envelope out of his pocket, dumping its powdery contents in Harry's coffee.

"What are you doing?" Gail gasped.

"Sleeping pills. I've been saving mine for a couple of weeks—you'll never know what I've gone through every night! I ground them up so they'll dissolve quickly. Harry is one of those people, as you may have noticed, who dump in about five spoonfuls of sugar, so he'll never know the difference."

"But, Vince! How do you know how much to give him? It might be an overdose! You don't want to kill him!"

"I know what I'm doing," Vince said impatiently. "He'll just sleep about six hours or so—I hope."

Harry came back and handed Vince the glasses.

"Thank you, Harry."

Gail watched in fascination while Harry spooned sugar into his coffee and carefully stirred it up. How could he stand it so sweet? Then he picked up the cup and took a large swallow. She held her breath, but he didn't change expression.

"Just right," he remarked and drank down the rest of it.

Usually, while Vince napped in the afternoon, Harry would take a run into town to do whatever shopping he needed to do for himself or errands for the household. Today, of course, he didn't leave, because he had been instructed by Leo not to leave the house until Leo returned.

Instead, he went into his own room and stretched out on his bed with a magazine.

In about half an hour Vince called up the stairs to Gail: "You can bring your things down now. He's out like a light."

She struggled down the stairs with her luggage and put her things down in the hall. Then she went back to take a look at Harry. She was still worried about him. He seemed to be sleeping very soundly, but was breathing normally.

"Are you sure he's all right?" she asked uncertainly.

"Of course. He's a big, powerful man, and I didn't give him all that much."

"Have you written the note you were going to leave?" she asked. "You know—telling Harry where to pick up the car."

"I've changed my mind about that," Vince said. "I'm not going to leave a note. Too risky in case Harry wakes up sooner than I expect. I'll call from the airport instead—just before we board the plane."

"What time does it leave?" she asked. "Did you make reservations?"

"Six o'clock," he told her. "A night flight to Paris. We can fly down to Cannes from there."

"Do they have flights to Paris from Fort Myers?"

"Of course—it's an international airport, isn't it?"

"I don't think so, not yet."

"Oh, we'll have to fly to Miami first, I guess. Yes, I believe that's what the girl said. Never mind—we'll get it straightened out when we get there."

It worried Gail that he seemed so vague about it, but he must know what he was doing, she thought. He had put on a very natty-looking beige summer suit with a yellow shirt. And he had only one bag ready to go.

"Is that all you're taking?" she asked. "What about all your other clothes?"

"I haven't time to pack everything," Vince said. "They can send it to me later. Don't quibble so much, my dear. Go get Harry's car and bring it around the front. He always leaves his keys in it. Then we'll get the bags in."

She went out to the garage, found the keys in the ignition, as Vince had said, and backed it out slowly.

Once the bags were stowed in the rear, Vince climbed in beside Gail. "We did it!" he exclaimed.

She drove off with many misgivings. But he did have every right to control his own destiny, as she had told herself so many times. There was no reason for him to be treated like a prisoner.

In a good mood, Vince was quite talkative and rambled on about his past adventures.

They got through Naples and went on north.

"Did you pack the memoirs and everything?" Vince asked her for at least the third time.

"Yes, Vince," Gail replied patiently. "When we get to Fort Myers, will you be able to direct me to the airport? I hope you're familiar with the area."

"Oh, I'm sure there'll be signs," he replied vaguely.

"How far is it?"

"Maybe forty miles, give or take a few." He looked at her with an odd, almost furtive expression that gave her another pang of misgiving. What was he up to now?

"Gail, I hope you won't mind, but I changed my mind about flying out tonight. I didn't want to tell you before, in case you were opposed to the idea. But I want to spend a night at a certain hotel before we continue on."

She gave him a glance of astonishment. "But the reservations—"

"They're for tomorrow afternoon. Not today."

She was too surprised to say anything more for a moment. Then she asked: "Where is this hotel —in Fort Myers?"

"No—on Sanibel Island. You know—it's called the Shell Island, because people go there to collect—"

"Yes, Vince, I've heard of it. But how far away is it?"

"Not far from Fort Myers. I'll show you where to turn off. Beautiful place. At least it used to be."

"But, Vince—why do you want to go there? I thought you wanted to get away as fast as possible. When Harry wakes up—"

"Oh, they'll never find us," he interrupted quickly. "I'll register under an assumed name. We could even leave the car there tomorrow and take a taxi to the airport. Yes, that would be a good idea. Save you driving, and throw them off our trail, if they're checking the airports. I can call them just before we board the plane, as I said before, and tell them where the car is."

"You say 'them,' but only Harry is there, Vince."

"Well, as soon as he wakes up and finds us and his car gone, he's sure to call Leo. Leo left him a number, of course, for the place where he'll be staying. No doubt he'll come home right away."

"But isn't that all the more reason to fly out before he gets here?"

"Not really. He'll check the airports first thing. It might be better, anyway, to wait until tomorrow."

His logic didn't quite make sense to Gail, but suddenly she realized that this development suited her very well. She knew now why she felt so miserable. It wasn't because she was helping Vince get away from Leo—she still felt that was justified. It was the knowledge that she shouldn't have gone off and left Harry in that condition.

You could die from an overdose of sleeping pills, and Vince was no expert on how many a person could safely take. It had looked like a very strong dose Vince had dumped in Harry's coffee. And if Harry died, she would never forgive herself.

Why, it would make her an accessory to his murder! Harry might be rather strange, but he was still a human being, and she couldn't bear it if he died. Somehow she had to make sure he was found as soon as possible. Even now it might be too late.

"All right, Vince," she said, "we'll go to your island."

Vince brightened considerably at this easy victory. "It's a place I went once with Elsa," he told her, the faraway look coming into his eyes. "In the early days of our marriage—a time of happiness and peace, lost now behind years of aimless living. I know that I can never recapture that lost beauty, but just once more before I die I want to go back and pay homage to that memory. You do understand, my dear?"

"Yes, Vince, I understand."

"In those days you could only reach Sanibel by boat. Now there's a causeway. I daresay it's been built up a lot since then. At least the hotel is still there—I looked it up in the phone book."

"Did you make reservations?"

"No, I didn't think that was necessary. The season is practically over now, and most of the winter people have gone."

When they reached Sanibel, Vince was dismayed by the sight of high rises.

"Dear, dear, look what they've done to it! Sanibel used to be such a lovely, quiet little island. The worst thing they ever did was to build that causeway."

Gail refrained from reminding him that was also true of his own island, and that he was responsible.

"Well, we're near the south end of the island here," Vince told her. "There's a four-way intersection up ahead. Turn right there on Periwinkle —that's the road that runs the length of the island—and keep going until I show you where to turn in."

It occurred to Gail that he seemed to know the island rather well for one who hadn't been there for decades, but she didn't say anything.

The hotel turned out to be an elderly pink stucco building built in the early Florida boom style: imitation Moorish architecture. Years had mellowed it and the grounds were spacious and beautifully landscaped.

"At least it hasn't changed," Vince said with satisfaction.

Gail pulled into the parking lot. A sign proclaimed this to be the Paradise Hotel.

"Just our flight bags, I think," Vince said. "We can leave the suitcases in the trunk. Unless there's something you need."

"No, that's all right."

The lobby was huge with comfortable groupings of coffee tables, chairs, and couches. Vince approached the desk with authority.

"I need two rooms, perhaps a suite if you have one, for myself and my daughter," he told the clerk, a small dark man with a thin moustache.

Gail was amused at the designation of daughter. Granddaughter would have been more like it, she thought, but Vince would never have put himself into that category.

"We're rather full at the moment, sir," the man told him with a speculative glance at Gail, "but there is a suite on the fourth floor—two bedrooms, two baths, and a small sitting room."

"Good—we'll take it," Vince told him and signed the card the man handed him.

An elderly bellboy took their flight bags and conducted them up in an equally old elevator to the fourth floor.

Gail sank into an easy chair with a sigh of relief.

"What name did you use?" she asked when the bellboy had gone.

"Vance and Elsa Stanford," he told her. "Always better to keep one's own initials. Not that it matters."

"I don't think the clerk thought we were related," she said.

Vince shrugged. "It's only for a night, and you'll never see him again. Do you mind?"

"Not really." She looked around the room, which was pleasant though not luxurious.

Vince sank down on the couch looking suddenly very weary. She got up and went over to him with a worried frown.

"I'm afraid the long drive was too much for you, Vince. You'd better rest now."

"You sound just like Harry," he complained wryly, "but, yes, I am a bit tired, and I will take a rest before dinner. I'm used to having my nap in the afternoon."

She followed him into his bedroom, opening his flight bag and finding the heart pills she knew he always took every afternoon. She'd given them to him a couple of times when Harry had a day off. He took off his jacket and shoes and settled down on the bed.

"Thank you, dear," he said. "We'll have dinner around eight. You run along now and have a drink or something and look the place over if you like."

Gail went to her own room where she laid out the things she'd need for the night, then looked speculatively at the telephone on the stand beside her bed. With the sitting room between them, he couldn't hear anything. She got an outside line, then dialed the number of the Sand Dollar's office. Fortunately, it was Judy who answered.

"Judy—this is Gail."

"Gail, where are you?"

"Believe it or not, in a hotel on Sanibel. Vince

decided to spend a night here before going on to the airport tomorrow. For old times' sake, or something."

"Is everything all right?"

"Yes. Vince got a bit tired, but he's resting now. Judy—will you do me a tremendous favor?"

"Of course, honey—anything humanly possible."

"In order to get away, Vince gave Harry a dose of sleeping pills. He said he knew what he was doing, but I've been worrying about it ever since. Could you possibly get off now and go over to Samburan and check on him? If he's still asleep —call a doctor."

"I wondered how you got away from Harry. Well, he's probably all right, but I will go over and check right away. I don't suppose the house is locked."

"No, we left the house and gate open. You can drive right in."

"Shall I call you back and report?"

Gail thought about it. "No, I'd better call you. In about an hour."

"Okay. Where are you, Gail? I ought to know —just in case I have to get hold of you in a hurry. I won't tell anyone."

"It's an old hotel called the Paradise. Oh, and ask for Elsa Stanford. Vince didn't sign our real names. We have a big suite on the fourth floor."

Judy chuckled. "Sounds naughty. I—oh, oh!"

"What do you mean, oh, oh?"

"Speaking of the devil—you can scratch that rescue mission, m'dear. Our Harry just walked in, very much alive, with fire in his eyes!"

"Judy! Don't tell him where we are!"

"No way, baby. I wouldn't put that thug on

your tail even if he tortured me with red hot pincers! I'll tell him your plane left for Europe an hour ago. Got to hang up now, he's heading this way."

Gail slowly put down the receiver. She was enormously relieved to know that Harry was all right, but alarmed that he was out trying to find them. Probably he thought Judy might know something. Well, he'd never find them here. How could he? She got up and went downstairs to get something cold to drink.

Vince seemed all right when he woke up and insisted on going down to the dining room for dinner instead of having it in their suite. He ordered a bottle of champagne with their meal.

And when she reminded him that he wasn't supposed to have any alcohol, he said airily: "A little champagne never hurt anyone, and this is supposed to be a celebration. They wouldn't let me have any at my birthday party, and that was ridiculous." He lifted his glass to hers. "To freedom!" he cried.

There was a look in his eyes that bothered her—a look of secret anticipation—but of what? Of his return to Europe?

Gail's uneasiness increased. She drank more champagne than she really wanted simply to keep Vince from drinking it, and when he would have ordered another bottle, she flatly refused.

"No, Vince. You promised me you'd be very careful if I helped you get away. Remember, we have to fly out tomorrow. No more drinking."

He ate very little of the excellent meal. And as soon as they had finished, he said that he was going up to bed. Well, that was good, she thought with relief. He went back upstairs and she took a walk in the garden behind the hotel. It was fragrant with flowers and the moon was out and she had an unbearable ache in her heart when she thought of Leo.

Finally, she decided there was no point in wandering around by herself, so she, too, went up to her room. After all, she hadn't slept much the night before, and she felt both physically and emotionally exhausted. She'd put a paperback in her flight bag, as she always did, so she showered, put on her pajamas, and lay on her bed with the book.

Then Gail found she couldn't concentrate and the print blurred before her eyes. She switched on the TV, then promptly switched it off again, because it was nothing but meaningless nonsense. She craved sleep, but knew that her nervous tension would keep her awake.

Perhaps, she thought, she should check on Vince, make sure that he was all right, that he had taken his bedtime medicine. Would he take a sleeping pill tonight or had he given them all to the unfortunate Harry? If he had any extras, she might borrow one rather than face another restless, miserable night.

Gail went into the sitting room where the lamp was still on and opened the door to Vince's bedroom. She saw his bed was empty.

Then a sound from the balcony made her turn swiftly. The French windows were partly open and she could see the little table and chairs out there. On the table was a bottle of whiskey, more than half empty. And beyond that, leaning against the railing, was Vince with a glass in his hand. He hadn't even undressed yet.

"Vince!" she called sharply. "What are you doing?"

He turned from the railing to look at her, and she saw that the excited gleam in his eyes had intensified into a strange, wild glare like that of a cornered animal.

"Natalie!" he said. "I told you to stop spying on me!"

"I'm not Natalie," she protested. "I'm Gail, and you know you shouldn't be drinking!"

He swallowed the rest of the liquid in the glass in one gulp and threw the glass over the railing. Gail heard a faint tinkle as it broke on the stone terrace far below.

"Liar!" Vince screamed. "They sent you, didn't they—sent you to spy on me! Then you'll tell them where I am and they'll come and get me! Well, I won't go back to that place, I tell you—I'd rather be dead!" He turned and put one leg over the railing.

"Vince!" Gail ran over to grab him around the waist. "Stop it! Nobody is going to hurt you! Listen to me—"

She had thought that he was frail and weak from his long illness, but his strength was unbelievable as he struggled to free himself from her grasp, his face contorted with terror.

Somehow he managed to get his other leg over so that he was sitting on the railing. Then he simply started sliding over and she felt herself being pulled with him. She continued to hang onto him, screaming for help, and felt the railing cut into her waist. She tried to get her feet braced against the bottom rail, but he still continued to slide slowly away from her.

His weight and the pull on her arms was unbearable—but she couldn't let go—it was all her fault. If he died, she had killed him!

"Leo!" she cried. "Oh, Leo—help me!" And she was falling over, head downward, her arms still around the old man's waist.

CHAPTER FIFTEEN

Suddenly, unbelievably, Leo and Harry were there and strong arms were grasping Gail and Vince, pulling them up to safety.

A distraught desk clerk was standing behind them, wringing his hands and moaning, "Oh, dear, oh, dear, whatever is going on here!"

"Send for an ambulance!" Leo snapped at him, and the man scurried off.

They carried Vince in and put him on the bed. He no longer put up any resistance; he seemed to be unconscious.

"Is he dead?" Gail cried in anguish.

Harry was taking his pulse. "No, just passed out." He gave her a dirty look. "Nice trick, doping my coffee."

"I didn't know he was going to do that."

171

"Oh, never mind." He grinned down at Vince. "The sly old fox! Never thought he could do it."

Leo was regarding Gail with some concern. "Are you all right?"

"Yes, I'm fine," she said and quietly fainted.

Much later at the hospital in Fort Myers, after having been checked over by a doctor and pronounced unharmed except for a badly bruised midriff and slight shock, Gail sat in a little room at one end of the hospital corridor with Leo and waited for the verdict on Vince. Harry prowled restlessly up and down the hall.

"What can I say, except to tell you how terribly sorry I am?" she said. "I've been a fool."

"Oh, he's conned the best of them," Leo replied with a smile. "It wasn't really your fault. I should have told you the truth instead of giving you vague warnings. But, you see, I promised Vince not to tell anyone on the island about his problems if he'd just come there with me for a good rest. They told me at the sanatorium that he'd be all right if he'd just keep away from alcohol. But the trouble was, he didn't really want to be cured. All he did was scheme how to get away and start drinking again."

"There's so much I don't understand," she said wearily.

"I know. It's a long story, but there's no need to go into all of it. Some people just can't seem to cope with having too much money dropped into their laps. Ever since his father died and he got the so-called Shane fortune, he's been going steadily downhill. Drinking, gambling, bad marriages."

"But his marriage to Elsa was happy, wasn't it? I thought it was her death that started his troubles, not the inheritance."

"Oh, that was part of it, I suppose. But before he met her, he'd been pretty wild. And the marriage was over so quickly—who knows what might have happened if she'd lived?"

"He said they'd been here together and it had been so lovely, such a happy, peaceful time."

"That was nonsense. Elsa was never in Florida. But Uncle used to come over here a lot in the old days. I guess he thought it would be a good spot to hole up for his drinking spree."

"How did you find us so quickly? Judy was going to tell Harry we'd already left for Europe."

"Yes, she did. But he'd already called me and I drove home as fast as I could. I knew you couldn't have flown anywhere because Uncle didn't have any money except for the fifty dollars he stole out of Harry's wallet. That wouldn't even have paid his bill at the hotel. No, I knew he must have gone to a hotel somewhere, so I went to Judy myself, explained the situation, and asked her to tell me where you were if she knew. So, of course, she told me."

"If you hadn't come just when you did—" Gail shuddered. "Oh, Leo, it was so horrible! And all my fault."

He took her hand. "No, it wasn't. Don't think about it. We did reach you in time."

"He said we'd go to Cannes to stay with a friend, and I was to finish the memoirs," she went on tearfully.

"Just more of his fantasy. He's flat broke except for the allowance Elizabeth and I give him.

There is no friend in Cannes or anywhere else. For some time now he's either been with Mother and me in Sweden or in and out of various hospitals. Left to himself, he starts drinking and goes out of his head."

"But the Shane fortune—"

"Doesn't exist. Never was as big as people here thought. A lot of it was lost long ago in the big crash. Before he died, my grandfather changed his will. I think he was sorry he'd disinherited my father. And he left Uncle the island and about a million dollars in bonds. The rest went into a trust fund for me. I was just a baby then."

"But surely Vince couldn't run through all that!"

"He did, though. Some of it went to his ex-wives. The rest was lost in gambling and extravagant living. Why do you think he sold half the island? He was going to sell the whole thing, but after he'd sold half of it, I stepped in and made him sell me the rest, the part with the house on it. I used part of Grandfather's money for it; it seemed fitting. He had loved Samburan and wouldn't have wanted it destroyed."

"But Vince keeps saying that Samburan is his—"

"He doesn't know truth from fantasy anymore. I let him think so if it makes him happy. He always could lie very charmingly."

"He really seemed to go crazy after he'd been drinking for a while. He thought I was someone called Natalie, sent to spy on him. How long has he been like that?"

"Well, he always drank a lot, but for years he could handle it fairly well. It just gradually started getting worse. But it's only been in the past five years or so that he gets really wild when he drinks. Now it doesn't take much to set him off—that's why we have to watch him so closely. Since the money he got for the island was gone, Elizabeth and I have been supporting him. She feels responsible; her own parents are dead and he's all she's got.

"We've tried to get him to quit drinking, but he didn't seem to want to. But after he had the mild heart attack, he got scared, thought he was going to die, I suppose. He seemed so sincere about reforming that I thought it would be safe to bring him here for a while."

"It might have been all right, if only I hadn't believed him—"

"He'd have found some other way. Don't blame yourself."

"But I do, Leo—if he dies—"

"Here comes the doctor now." Leo got to his feet and went to meet the man who was walking toward them.

"He'll be fine," the doctor assured them. "I've got him sedated now, and he'll sleep it off. Oddly enough, it didn't bring on another heart attack. He's a tough old bird." He grinned at them. "But he'll have to stop drinking—permanently."

Leo heaved a deep sigh. "Thank heaven he's all right. Thank you, Doctor. Could I see him now?"

"I'm afraid you'll have to wait for morning when he wakes up."

"How long will he have to stay in the hospital?"

"Maybe only a day for observation. We'll see. He won't feel very good for a few days, though, and you'd better keep him in bed. Goodnight. I'll see you tomorrow." He hurried down the corridor.

Leo turned to Gail, who was crying quietly. "Everything's going to be all right," he said. "I'll have Harry take you home, and I'll stay until Uncle can leave. You must be exhausted. We have both cars here at the hospital, and Harry brought all your things from the hotel. I know you wouldn't want to go back there."

"No—never! But, Leo—I think since I've got all my things, I'd better just go on to the airport and take the next plane out. You don't want me at Samburan."

He cupped her chin in his hand and gazed into her sorrowful dark eyes.

"Gail, ever since we met, we've been at cross purposes. Neither of us understood what the other was up to. We need to have a long talk and straighten everything out. And, of course, we want you at Samburan. Please come back."

So, of course, she went back to Samburan.

It was morning by the time Gail and Harry got there, and she slept most of the day, exhausted both physically and emotionally.

Vince and Leo came home the afternoon of the following day. Harry got him quickly to bed, fussing over him like a worried mother; apparently he had quite forgiven him for the powdered sleeping pills. Aside from being shaky and a bit drawn, Vince seemed none the worse for his little adventure. Before he took his nap, he asked Gail to come in and see him.

"Well, my dear," he said, taking her hand. "I made a nice mess of things, didn't I! I wonder if you can ever forgive me for using you as a pawn in my stupid little game."

"Of course, I'll forgive you, Vince," she said gently. "I understand how terrible a craving it must be. I guess nothing else seems to matter when you're in its clutches."

"Leo told me how you saved my life. If you hadn't hung on to me when I went over—"

"But he and Harry saved us both. Let's just forget it, Vince. I don't like to think about it."

"But I owe you a debt I can never repay. My life is worthless, but you are young with all yours ahead of you. To think that you were willing to sacrifice—"

"Vince—please don't talk about it anymore."

"All right, but I won't forget. I don't remember any of it, of course. I never do. I've done a lot of crazy things before, I suppose, but I've never endangered anyone else's life before. This time I really mean it, Gail, when I say I'll *never* take another drink. I swear to you, I do."

"I hope you mean that, Vince." She smiled at him pityingly, knowing that whatever he said, however sincere he was at the moment, he could never be trusted. It had gone on for too many years.

"The doctors told me I could be cured only if I wanted to be cured. I never did before. I preferred my old lifestyle. But that's over now. They also told me I had the constitution of an ox or I'd have been dead long ago. So maybe I'll survive long enough to get those memoirs written after all. What do you think, Gail? Are you still interested?"

"If we can work things out, yes, very much so. But now you must rest." She leaned over and kissed his cheek. "I'll see you later."

Tears came into his eyes. "God bless you, my dear," he murmured.

She went out and found Leo waiting for her. His eyes studied her face.

"Are you all right now, Gail?" he asked.

"Yes, quite all right." She put her hands on her waist with a grimace. "A bit stiff and sore here, that's all."

"Let's take a walk on the beach. If you feel up to it."

"Of course I do."

He took her hand and they walked to the cove.

"Vince seems very contrite, very subdued," she said. "Do you think he means it?"

"I've seen him like that before. He always means it at the time, but then he starts to get bored and we're back where we started. Oh, well. We can but hope. If I weren't so fond of him, I'd have given up on him long ago." He laughed. "He does have a way with him."

"He does, indeed."

They walked slowly along the beach with the sandpipers skittering ahead of them.

"He's agreed to go to the sanatorium in Denmark for a while," Leo told her. "He thinks he needs a longer drying-out period. After that, we'll see. I can visit him every week. It's a beautiful place, and they'll take good care of him."

"It sounds ideal."

"I had a long talk with him yesterday, Gail. He told me that he'd asked you to marry him and that you refused without a second's thought."

"Well, of course I couldn't marry him, Leo. In the first place, he didn't really want me to, you know. He just threw in the proposal as a sort of additional lure to get me to agree to take him away from Samburan. In the second place, I would never marry for convenience or money or any such thing."

Leo looked at her, the lights in his blue-green eyes glowing. "What sort of marriage do you want, Gail? If any."

She answered without hesitation: "A traditional marriage. A marriage based on love and respect and friendship. A forever sort of marriage with children and a real home."

"But I thought you were eager to go to a big city and work for a newspaper."

"I always thought I was. But when it came right down to making the break, I always dragged my feet. I made the excuse that my aunt needed me. She didn't. She leads a busy, happy life with lots of friends and a sister nearby. When I was in college, my journalism professor told me I'd never make the big time because, although I wrote well, I wasn't aggressive enough. I could never go for the jugular, as they like to say. That's true, Leo. I've done a lot of soul-searching since I came here, and I know now that I'm not really a career-woman type. I don't want to be alone—I want a family to love and to love me. Of course, I can always write, wherever I am." She stopped in confusion. Why was she saying all these things?

"And the memoirs," he said. "Are you still interested in them?"

"Oh, yes! Very much so. I would love to go on with them, but if Vince is going into a sanatorium, I don't see how—"

"Why not? If you were in Sweden, you could go over every week, as I said, and work with him. It

would be very good for him, I think. Give him
some incentive in life. And he is fond of you, you
know."

"But how could I live in Sweden? I—"

"There's plenty of room on the estate."

"But I thought you wanted me to stay here and
do it by long distance."

"That was when I still thought you were after
Uncle. I wanted to separate you from him, but I
didn't want you entirely out of my life." He
pulled her into his arms. "Gail, darling, darling,
don't you know how I've felt from the beginning?"

She managed to pull away. "Wait, Leo!" she
gasped. "We haven't finished talking yet. You
said we needed to straighten everything out, and
we do!"

"I'm straightened out!"

"Well, I'm not! What about Elizabeth?"

"What about her?" he asked.

"Aren't you still in love with her?"

He laughed. "We haven't been in love for many
years. We thought we were once when we were
very young, but it was only because we were
thrown so closely together. We soon found out it
was a mistake and broke the engagement. We're
still good friends, though, in a cousinly sort of
way. She adores her Hungarian husband, and I
don't think she'll ever divorce him, no matter
how often she threatens to."

He paused. "But there is still one thing that
puzzles me, come to think of it."

"What's that, Leo?"

"That night on the boat you really seemed to
care about me, and then in the morning you had
changed, were cold and unfriendly. What happened?"

"Oh, that! Elfie told me she heard her mother telling you to get me away from Vince even if you had to romance me yourself. So I thought that's why you were doing it, and naturally I wasn't overjoyed."

"Oh, Gail! Surely you don't think I'm the sort of man who would—"

"Not anymore, but I did then. Just as you thought I was the sort who would marry an old man for his money."

He grinned ruefully and pulled her into his arms again.

"My darling," he mumbled. "I think it's about time that you and I get better acquainted."

"Yes, Leo," she agreed. "Oh, yes!"